The Fed

On the far side of the house, almost nothing remained but hints of the stone foundations. A halo of rubble ringed the scene: shattered timbers and fragments of masonry radiated out from the ruins like the rays on a child's drawing of the sun.

In 1918, Roland had marched through Château-Thierry with Pershing, during the Second Battle of the Marne. The little village had been blown apart by German and Allied artillery in the war's last gasp, but Pine Beach was in even worse shape. The far side of the house looked shorn off rather than blown up: it was reduced to a couple of courses of stone, surrounded by a wide ring of debris.

Boot prints and tire tracks on the muddy ground reminded him that the scene was far from pristine. He turned to Sheriff Engle. "Where were the bodies?"

The sheriff stretched out his arms in an all-encompassing gesture. "All over," he said. "A few were whole, some were in pieces, some were…"

"Some were what?"

"Hard to describe. Crushed, I guess. Like a bug when you step on it and drag your shoe."

To Jamie Davis, my love, my friend, and my partner in crime.

Cover illustration by Shane Pierce.

Color insert artwork by Anthony Devine and David Griffith.

ISBN: 978-1-63344-313-6

Printed in China.

Fantasy Flight Games
1995 West County Road B2
Roseville, MN 55113
USA

Find out more about Fantasy Flight Games
and our many exciting worlds at

www.FantasyFlightGames.com

An

Novella

The Dirge of Reason

by Graeme Davis

Fantasy Flight Games

Welcome to Arkham

IT IS THE HEIGHT OF THE ROARING TWENTIES. Flappers and young fellas dance the Charleston at raucous jazz clubs gleaming bright with electric lights. Beneath this gilded glamour, bloody turf wars rage, funded by gangsters and crooked cops who frequent rival speakeasies and gambling dens.

Amid these changing times, old New England towns hold their secrets close. Off the Aylesbury pike, in reclusive Dunwich, rolling hills hide decrepit farms and witch-haunted hollows. Past Cape Ann, the remote fishing village of Innsmouth rots from within. At the mouth of the Miskatonic River, mist-shrouded Kingsport lies dreaming. All the while, historic Arkham broods on the upper banks of the Miskatonic, its famed university delving into the world's darkest, most ancient mysteries.

Arkham's citizens insist everything is normal in their sleepy town, but horrific and bizarre events occur with increasing frequency. Strange lights flicker and people disappear in the forest beyond Hangman's Brook. Misshapen silhouettes prowl graveyards and shorelines, leaving savaged corpses in their wake. Nightmarish artifacts and disturbing tomes have surfaced, chronicling gods and incantations the world has tried to forget. Cavalier scientists have glimpsed far-flung worlds beyond our own that shatter the known laws of reality. Are these events somehow connected? If so, what calamity do they portend?

Those who dare investigate these incidents witness the inexplicable. Having seen such phenomena, they can never regain their old view of the world. Now that they know the hideous truth, they cannot run or hide from it. Just beneath the reassuring veneer of reality—a veneer that was never meant to be worn away—are forces that can drive the average person to despair. Yet, a rare few try to avert the end of the world, knowing it may well cost them their lives or sanity.

These investigators must rely on their wits and skills to learn as much as they can before it's too late. Some may find courage in the grace of a rosary, while others may burn away their fears with a swig of bootleg whiskey. They must try their hand at unpredictable spells that could doom them, or take up rifles and revolvers to combat foul creatures plaguing the night. Will it be enough?

Chapter 1

Arkham's dark and pillared police station loomed over the city with what seemed like a disdainful frown. The desk sergeant looked up at Agent Roland Banks with much the same expression when the agent presented his credentials.

"Bureau of Investigation, huh?" He cast a jaundiced eye over Roland's badge. "Well, la-di-da."

"I'm looking for—," Roland glanced down at his notebook, "—Sheriff Engle of the Miskatonic County Sheriff's Office."

The old bull's expression turned half a shade more sour. "I bet you are. That society dame send you?"

"The Bureau sent me."

"Well, hurrah for J. Edgar Hoover. Down the hall, turn left."

Following the sergeant's directions, Roland passed through a glass door with the name of the sheriff's office on the outside in gold letters, and found himself in a narrow lobby with a door on either side and a small desk at which a middle-aged woman sat reading a dime novel. He stood and waited while she finished her paragraph, turned down the corner of her page, and closed the book before looking up at him.

"Can I help you?" Her tone suggested that she would prefer not to.

Roland presented his badge again and was about to ask for Sheriff Engle when the door on the left opened and a head stuck itself out.

"That's all right, Myrna," the man said. "This will be the federal agent we're expecting." He turned to Roland. "Am I right?"

"Agent Roland Banks, Bureau of Investigation."

"Pleased to meet you, Agent Banks. Come on in." Sheriff Engle retreated back through the door, beckoning Roland to follow him.

The office was almost as small as the lobby. Sheriff Engle waved Roland to a chair and edged to his own seat around a desk the size of a matchbox. The desk and the windowsill were piled with papers, and the sheriff hunted through them as he spoke.

"So what did they tell you in Boston?"

"Not much," said Roland. "Just to come here and talk to you. Something about a house that was destroyed. They weren't big on details." His stop in Boston had been brief. After a day on the train from Virginia, he had been rushed off to Arkham before his half-finished coffee had stopped steaming. The questions he tried to ask had brought the kind of silence that filled an Irish pub right after someone ordered a black and tan.

"Well, welcome to Arkham." There was just a trace of irony in Sheriff Engle's voice. "We've been expecting you."

"You have? I wasn't even expecting me before yesterday."

The sheriff chuckled. "Oh, it was inevitable," he said. "I take it you never met Mrs. van Dreesen?"

Roland shook his head. "Never had the pleasure."

Roland did not need to meet Mrs. van Dreesen. A Photostat copy of her letter to the Bureau higher-up sat in his valise along with a few other papers they had given him in Boston. From the letter's familiar tone, it was clear that Mrs. van Dreesen was a friend of the higher-up's wife, and it did not take a Fed to know that the higher-up would know no peace, either social or domestic, until the matter was resolved to Mrs. van Dreesen's complete satisfaction. She even wrote in a Knickerbocker drawl.

"She thought we local bumpkins were in over our heads," the sheriff went on, "and she let us know it loudly and repeatedly. I was half expecting J. Edgar Hoover in person."

"No," said Roland, "just me."

"I've got everything here," said Sheriff Engle, tapping a fat stack of paper into shape. "Our report on the scene, copies of correspondence between Mrs. van Dreesen and her insurance company, and the cable from New York telling us to expect an agent."

Roland took the proffered stack and glanced at the telegram on the top. It bore the same name as the memo in his valise: the name that had made him look twice. He started to turn over the papers as they talked. "I'll be sure to look all of this over," he said. "In the meantime, can you give me the headlines?"

The sheriff leaned back in his chair and counted off points on his fingers. "Pine Beach," he said. "A posh lake house outside of town on Chaumadgee Lake, owned by Mrs. Edgar van Dreesen—first name Edith—of Manhattan, New York. About sunset on the fifteenth, it was destroyed. The ground shook as far as here in town, and the noise was heard over two miles away. Thirty-eight people died."

"Thirty-eight? Was it a house party?"

"No—an orchestra."

"A what?"

"It's all in the notes," Sheriff Engle said. "Mrs. van Dreesen was a patron, and she lent the house to the orchestra for rehearsals. They were due to open in Boston this week."

"But the house blew up first."

"That's right."

"So Mrs. van Dreesen lost more than just a house. She lost an orchestra, too."

"Right again."

"I'm not a society type, but I imagine that would be embarrassing."

"No doubt."

"So it was an explosion?"

"Most likely. But here's the kicker: we can't figure out how it blew up. The gas lines don't run that far into the country, and the house wasn't fitted for propane. It did have a boiler for hot water, but that was wood-fired, and I doubt that even the *Mauretania* has a boiler big enough to blow up with that much force. I was starting to look at the orchestra when my office got orders to do nothing further until you arrived. My guess is, there are things about the orchestra she didn't want coming out. They were a pretty rowdy crew."

"Rowdy? What kind of orchestra was it? Jazz?"

The sheriff looked surprised at the question. "Not jazz," he said. "The papers call them *avant-garde*, whatever that means. What are you thinking?"

"If no one else was there, that makes them suspects as well as victims," said Roland. "*Avant-garde*, you said—so they were artsy types?" Roland waited for Sheriff Engle to nod. "Did they cause any trouble in town?"

"Not in town so much, but they weren't popular with their neighbors. One time they found a dead raccoon and stole someone's motorboat to give it a Viking funeral."

"So they were probably not too concerned about Prohibition?"

"We did have to lock a couple of them up for public drunkenness, but I never did find out where they were getting their booze from." Sheriff Engle's answer was just a little too quick for Roland's liking. "How does that fit with the house blowing up?"

"Could they have been running a still in the house? I've seen a still explosion take down a good-sized cabin."

"You wouldn't ask that if you knew the house. I doubt the DuPont chemical company has a still big enough to do that kind of damage. The place was more like a mansion than a cabin."

"What does that leave? Dynamite? Bootleggers, maybe?"

Sheriff Engle ran a hand over his mustache. "I couldn't say. We've never had anything like that out here before. I guess that's one reason Mrs. van Dreesen wanted the Bureau involved. She didn't seem to have much faith in us locals."

"I'm sorry to hear that," Roland said, "although you seem to be taking it well."

The sheriff raised an eyebrow. "I am?"

"Better than any local officer I've ever met before, in fact. Most people in your position don't like getting the high hat from some society type and having to hand over a case to the Feds. How come you're so calm about it?"

Sheriff Engle gave a quick bark of laughter. "I would not presume to comment on my betters," he said. "Mrs. van Dreesen felt that the case was beyond the expertise of the local authorities, and I was forced to agree."

Roland hunted through the stack for a letter he had glimpsed and held it up to the sheriff.

"Because of this?" The typed sheet had the letterhead of the New Netherland Insurance Company, and the letter began, "We regret to inform you…"

"That's right. I wasn't able to assign a definite cause, so the insurance company ruled it an act of God and refused to pay out. That led, from what I heard, to a spirited discussion by telephone, which led in turn—"

"Let me guess," said Roland. "It led to me."

Sheriff Engle replied with an apologetic shrug. "The next day, I got a call from the Bureau telling me to stop everything and wait for you to get here."

Roland heaved a weary sigh. "Of course you did," he said. "And if Mrs. van Dreesen doesn't like the report I turn in…"

The sheriff nodded in mock sadness. "That's about the size of it."

"No wonder you've been such a model of cooperation," Roland said. "You couldn't wait to offload this case onto some other poor sap, could you?" Sheriff Engle made no reply. "Is that why you were so quick to reach no conclusion?"

The sheriff leaned back and ran a hand through his hair. "Look, Agent Banks," he said, "I've got nothing against you. I know there's a long and noble tradition of federal agencies swooping in and stealing cases from us honest, hard-working, local bulls, and sure, maybe some might think it's cute to hand a poisoned chalice off to the G-men, but I'm not one of them."

"How do I know that?"

"You don't know it, and that's why I'm telling you. Now, Arkham may look like a sleepy little place, but it has its share of troubles—more than its share sometimes. If I can clear a case by myself, I do it. Why? Because I don't need federal agents coming in and stirring up more trouble than they solve because they don't know anything about this city and its people. That's what you'll do, Agent Banks, whether you intend to or not. And if you think—"

"If I stir up trouble, Sheriff, it will be because there's trouble to stir up. The reason you locals don't like G-men is because G-men don't turn a blind eye to handshake deals or special arrangements."

"Sell it someplace else, Agent. You know, and I know, you're only here at all because of Mrs. van Dreesen's connections, so don't play the altar boy about influence and arrangements."

A long silence simmered as the two men glared at each other across the tiny desk. Finally, Roland spread his hands in surrender.

"All right," he said. "So we both know how the world works. And you're right—I don't know you. You don't know me, either, but the sooner I clear up this case, the sooner I can be gone—and believe me, I want that just as much as you do. No offense intended. I'm sure Arkham's a fine city."

"None taken," said Sheriff Engle with a slightly lopsided grin, "and for what it's worth, I wouldn't wish Mrs. van Dreesen on anyone—not even a Fed. If you have more luck figuring this out than I did, I'll be very happy about it. So what do you say?" He stood and held out his hand. After a moment, Roland shook it.

"I'm sorry." He sat back down. "It's been a long couple of days getting here. I may have brought some old frustrations with me."

"Two days?" The sheriff looked surprised. "I was told to expect someone from Boston."

Roland let out a short, bitter laugh. "Oh, I was in Boston—for about fifteen minutes. They couldn't wait to get rid of me. I got the impression Arkham was catching, somehow."

"It does have a certain reputation," Sheriff Engle admitted. "The whole valley does, going back to the witch times. Somehow, we can't seem to shake it off. So where did they send you from?"

"Virginia," Roland replied.

"Let me guess: you were chasing bootleggers all over Hillbilly Holler, and you ran smack into one of those handshake deals you were talking about. So Mrs. van Dreesen is your punishment?"

Roland gave a weary nod. Everyone knew that the BOI had spent the last couple of years in near-constant territorial skirmishes with almost every other federal agency. Director Hoover made no secret of the fact that he wanted to bury the memories of corruption and botched investigations like the Teapot Dome scandal. Since Hoover trusted only himself and the agents under his direct command, conflict with other agencies was inevitable. In Jubal County, the other agency was the Bureau of Internal Revenue's Prohibition Unit. The two government agencies hated each other worse than the bootleggers did.

Roland had never been good at politics. He had never wanted to be. Hoover's anti-corruption stance was what had attracted him to the BOI in the first place: putting bad guys away rather than wasting energy plotting against people who were supposed to be on his own side. Some of the other agents laughed behind his back—called him naïve, a Boy Scout. But no one could get anything on him if there was nothing to get, and that was the only way to avoid being dragged into the mire.

His Boy Scout policy had hit the rocks in a cat's cradle that went by the name of Jubal County. Everyone there was a cousin or an in-law to everyone else, and no one liked outsiders. At some point, someone in one of the federal agencies had made a deal with someone in Jubal County, and the Boy Scout had blundered in and ruined something for someone. Nothing had been said, of course—these things were never openly acknowledged—but suddenly the Boston Field Office needed Agent Roland Banks and no one else would do.

Roland opened his mouth, then closed it, and finally sighed. "I shouldn't discuss Bureau cases with anyone outside the Bureau."

"You didn't. All I heard was you had a long journey."

Roland started to reply, but his stomach interrupted with a sound that bounced off the windows and made the sheriff's eyes widen.

"Don't tell me you haven't eaten yet?"

Roland shook his head. "I came here straight from the station. Professional courtesy: always announce yourself to local law enforcement right away."

The sheriff seemed amused. "I guess you are a by-the-book kind of fellow, aren't you? Well, no wonder you were a little bad tempered. Did you see Velma's on your way here?"

Roland nodded. "I could hardly miss it."

"That sign does catch the eye, doesn't it? It was the first neon in Arkham, believe it or not. Caused quite a fuss when Velma first put it up. Anyhow, why don't you come back in an hour or so, and you can tell me how you want to proceed? I can take you to the site—," he cast a glance out the window, "—and we might have a couple of hours of usable daylight left. Or you could get yourself situated, go through the files, and we could start out fresh in the morning. Just let me know."

Roland nodded his thanks and rose to leave.

"Don't miss the cherry pie," Sheriff Engle said in parting. "You've never had anything like it!"

Chapter 2

Roland shouldered through the door of the diner. His stomach gave a skip of joy as the comforting fug of coffee and grill-grease hit his nostrils.

Sheriff Engle clearly had not lied about the food. Roland counted two cops at the counter, two more at a table, and two ministers at another table. Dozens of diners in dozens of towns had taught Roland that uniforms and dog collars were two sure signs of good eating.

The cops at the counter gave him a slow once-over as he entered. They had pegged him for a G-man and they wanted him to know it. Roland returned a brief nod of professional courtesy and scanned the room for an empty table.

"Sit anywhere, hon! I'll be right with you!" A cheery woman with "Velma" stitched on her chest in red script smiled at him from behind the counter. By the time Roland reached the table he had picked, she was already pouring coffee. Roland waved the menu away and ordered steak, hash browns, and three eggs over easy. Then he took a long pull at his coffee and felt its warmth slide all the way down.

The cops at the nearby table gave him a cold stare of their own, like street-corner toughs glaring across an invisible line into rival turf. Roland shot them a beaming grin that stuck one toe over the line into sarcasm, and they turned away sulkily, just like countless other local cops had done before them in countless other towns.

Roland reached in his valise for the newspaper he had bought at the station and opened it on the table in front of him, eating one-handed as he read. The *Arkham Advertiser* was as parochial as its name suggested, but it was local news that Roland was after. The police files stayed out of sight, away from prying eyes. He wrote down the address of the paper's office: reporters were often better friends to federal agents than local law enforcement, especially if they thought a G-man could help take their local story national.

The front page was dominated by follow-up stories about Pine Beach: "Orchestra's Remains Shipped Home," ran the main headline. The newspaper named the thirty-eight casualties as members of the New England Virtuosi, plus a composer named Oliver Haldane.

An unnamed "New York correspondent" described the music world's shock at Haldane's sudden death and reprised several breathless rumors about composer and orchestra, full of bedroom antics, low company ranging from bootleggers to Surrealists to suspected Communists, and every other imaginable form of bad behavior. Mostly, the stories were about how well-connected the paper's correspondent was in New York's arts world, although there was a brief mention of "Arkham's own jazz joint, the Nightingale Club, in Uptown." Roland made a note of the name.

A piece on an inside page wondered whether the van Dreesens would rebuild and whether the summer's trade would be affected by the city's sudden notoriety. Although Arkham clearly was not as dependent on "summer people" as the Hamptons or Cape Cod, it seemed that they did bring welcome cash to the area.

The coverage was exactly what might be expected from a local rag. Roland noted down the names of the editor and a couple of reporters.

"You from out of town, hon?" It sounded like a question, but it was really a test. No stranger could pass unnoticed in a joint like this.

Roland lifted his freshly filled coffee cup, nodding his thanks to the waitress for the refill and for the heaping plate of food she had brought. "That's right," he said.

"A terrible thing, that fire." She heaved a brief, conventional sigh of sympathy, and when Roland did not correct her on the cause of the destruction, she went on with her probing. "So, are you press, insurance, or law?"

"Are those the only choices?"

Velma acknowledged his parry with a raised eyebrow and a low chuckle.

"They have been for the last week, I can tell you that," she said with a conspiratorial smile. "Besides, you don't have the look of an encyclopedia salesman." She glanced down at his valise. "Nor the case, either."

"Good eye. Are you sure you're not a detective yourself?"

Her smile broadened as Roland turned back to his food. Velma already knew he was a G-man—the cops' reactions would have told her even if the cops themselves had not—and from now on it would be a game to see how much she could get out of him. Gossip was currency in a place like this, and fresh gossip brought more customers than fresh coffee.

When Velma came by to take his empty plate and fill his coffee cup for a third time, Roland ordered the cherry pie. "The sheriff said I shouldn't miss it," he said. Velma beamed, and not just at the compliment.

"You're a lawman. I knew it!" she said.

"You knew it before I sat down. Any of the people from the house ever eat here?"

"Those musicians?" She made a face. "I threw a couple of them out when they first got here."

"They made trouble?"

"Not trouble, exactly—just annoyance. They were as drunk as a pair of skunks and wanting all kinds of things that aren't on the menu. Told them I'm not running a fraternity house and they should beat it and not come back. Never saw any of them again."

"What about the owners?"

"Mrs. van High-and-Mighty?" Velma snorted. "Imagine her here! For one thing I'm all out of lace tablecloths, and she'd never get the grease smell out of her ermine. She brought her own cook from New York when she came up here; that's what I heard. The summer people don't mix here, not like on the coast. Oh, the paper would mention some grand party or other—debutante balls and whatnot—but we never saw hide nor hair of them in town. Just their people, buying supplies and such."

Velma waited a couple of seconds with an expectant smile on her face, but when Roland offered nothing in return for her insights she turned away to another table. "You be sure and come back, now."

Roland finished his pie and coffee, and left a generous tip. He had got more out of Velma than he had expected to, although none of it was much help. Still, coffee and a hot meal had him feeling almost human again.

Roland returned to the police station and left a message for Sheriff Engle to meet him the following morning for a visit to Pine Beach. He was still bone-tired, and the site that had confounded the Miskatonic County Sheriff's Office would require all his faculties. Meanwhile, he had the stack of documents from the sheriff, plus whatever he could get from the newspaper office. Like a Boy Scout, he believed in being prepared.

With a full stomach and no need to rush, Roland took in more of the city as he headed for the newspaper office. The little square looked somehow different in the afternoon light. Roland noticed a dark, rough-looking stone at one side and a masonry arch marking the western entrance. A handful of locals lolled on benches or strolled across the square on various errands: it was a scene typical of countless small towns, but for some reason Roland felt uneasy.

Perhaps it was the grim, high-walled building that loomed behind the square. It had been unseen behind Roland as he had walked to the police station, but from this direction, it crouched over the city center like a great, grey beast, hunched and threatening. With its brick walls and its many roofs and chimneys, it might have been a cursed mansion from the mind of Edgar Allan Poe or someone similar.

From across the street, Roland read the sign "Arkham Sanatorium" over a sharp-looking wrought-iron fence. He had been to a few asylums in his time—bathtub gin rotted the brain as well as the gut—but he had never seen one so close to the center of a city—not outside of a Lon Chaney movie, at least. Together with the crooked roofs and shadowed alleys, it was easy to see how Arkham had acquired the sinister reputation of which Sheriff Engle had spoken.

After a quick stop at the newspaper office, Roland found a hotel downtown. The Excelsior looked as though it belonged in a larger city and had somehow wandered into Arkham by accident.

The glass panes in the hotel's double doors were etched with its name in an ornate script from the previous century. The lace curtains framing the windows might have been white once, but were now a color that a kindly disposed decorator might describe as ivory. The worn-looking, scarlet and gold carpet was covered by a broad runner of plain red that stretched between the doors and a front desk of wood and polished brass. It was not the Waldorf Astoria, but it would be tolerably clean, if not especially comfortable, and it would be within Roland's Bureau-mandated budget. He had stayed in far worse places.

The bell on the front desk summoned a tall, cadaverous-looking man whose remaining hair fell lank over one side of his head. Dressed in a frock coat and a Celluloid collar, he seemed like a relic from another age, although he complemented the genteel shabbiness of his hotel perfectly. He looked at Roland's badge with no change of expression and pulled a brown paper package from under the desk without comment.

The manager gave Roland a room on the second floor. Seeing no pen on the desk, Roland unscrewed the cap on his Sheaffer and opened the register. A familiar name made him pause and look more closely. Oliver Haldane had registered at the hotel, four months earlier. He spun the book around to face the manager.

"What can you tell me about this guest?" he asked. The manager's face went blank so fast that Roland could almost hear the sound of a door slamming.

"I'm sorry, sir." The voice was respectfully soft, but unyielding. "The hotel's policy does not permit—"

"This man is dead," Roland snapped, "and so are thirty-seven other people. A house was destroyed. I am a federal agent looking into those deaths. Would you like to reconsider the hotel's policy?"

The manager recoiled a hair, but his expression did not change.

"If you wish, I can refer you to the owners' attorneys," he said, "although I doubt anyone here will know anything of use to you. The staff of this hotel is under strict instructions to respect our guests' privacy."

It was clear from the manager's tone that nothing short of a federal warrant would budge him an inch further. Roland took his room key and went upstairs before he said anything he might regret. He was not the kind of agent who went around bullying civilians.

Roland spent the rest of the day going through Sheriff Engle's police file and the stack of notes, photographs, and back issues from the newspaper office. Along with the police report came several photographs, and Roland scoured them with a pocket lens until his eyes felt like sandpaper, but they told him next to nothing. The house had been big, which was hardly surprising, and had been built of timber on a stone foundation. A few older pictures showed it intact: three stories, the lower two enclosed by a broad, double-decked veranda-*cum*-balcony, with dormer windows in the roof and massive stone chimneys poking up like the stumps of primordial trees. A manicured lawn ran down to the beach that gave the house its name, with an Italian-looking fountain of pale stone adding an awkwardly formal touch to the New England woodsiness of the scene.

One photo, dated 1905, was captioned "Worthington-Mullen Wedding, Worthington House, Pine Beach, Arkham, Mass." Roland made a note to find out who the Worthingtons were, when the house was built, and when the van Dreesens bought it. Perhaps he might find a hint of some inherent instability in the construction or the underlying ground, which had caught up with the house and its occupants that night.

The recent photographs showed rubble and matchwood, and here and there a barely recognizable piece of a human body. It looked more like the result of an artillery bombardment than an accidental explosion. Roland laid the photographs of the intact house on the floor and tried to orient the scenes of destruction around them. He had half of the house to work with, as well as the fountain, which had been reduced to a stump. An ambiguous shadow extended behind it. The lawns were all but lost beneath a layer of debris that extended halfway to the lake.

The back numbers he had picked up at the newspaper office revealed even less. The same photographs were reproduced in grainy dots and credited to "E. Talbot." Roland flipped one of the prints over and found the same name rubber-stamped on the back in smudged blue ink, along with an address in New York. Another summer person—one unlikely to have stayed around after an experience like that. He wrote the address in his notebook.

There were a few stories about the orchestra, starting with a piece from several weeks ago, announcing that they would be coming to Pine Beach. As their patron, Mrs. van Dreesen received a respectful number of column inches, and Arkham congratulated itself on being ideally remote and peaceful, yet well-appointed, to attract a renowned orchestra wishing to rehearse an important new piece ahead of a New York premiere. Initially glowing with anticipation, the reports changed after the musicians arrived in Arkham. Now and again, as the sheriff had said, their drunken escapades had led to a night in the cells, but there was no mention of lawsuits or trials. The invisible hand of Mrs. van Dreesen at work, most likely: the rich, and the friends of the rich, could get away with a great deal.

Darkness fell, and Roland ordered food from the kitchen. He went over everything again, chewing on a paper-thin piece of cold roast beef between two dry, curled-up slices of bread. After another couple of hours, he opened a window and stuck his head out to get some air, focusing on a distant spire to give his eyes a break. Arkham was layer upon layer of shadows, one behind the other, like the set of a movie he had seen a few years ago, about a sleep-walker in a German town made up of crazy, jagged angles.

Moments later, or possibly minutes, he jerked awake just in time to stop himself from toppling out of the window. He was close to sleepwalking. He put the papers away and went to bed, very little the wiser.

Chapter 3

"Sleep well?"

Roland replied to the sheriff's cheery greeting with a noncommittal grunt. He had been with the Bureau so long that he could probably sleep on a bed of nails if he had to, but sleep had done nothing to relieve his frustration. Much of it, he admitted to himself, had little or nothing to do with Arkham or this case—he was just getting started, after all—and a lot more to do with Jubal County and his burning sense of the injustice he had suffered there. He climbed into the sheriff's car, hoping that a visit to the site would give him something to go on—or just something to occupy his mind.

Sheriff Engle drove out of town on the Gloucester Road. Dense woods blocked out the view on either side, just as they had on the train. Once again, Roland felt as though they were trying to close in on him.

"Did you get anything from the files?" Sheriff Engle asked.

"Just a headache," Roland replied. Sheriff Engle nodded sympathetically and kept driving.

"Explosion, cause unknown," Roland quoted. "Did you really expect anyone to be pleased with a conclusion like that?"

"No, I didn't," said the sheriff. "But it was say that or make something up—something I'd then have to defend in front of Mrs. van Dreesen, her insurance company, and probably a judge. I mean, thirty-eight deaths, New York society types—that's not the kind of thing that's going to go smoothly."

"Ain't that the truth," said Roland, "and you figured that whatever you said, Mrs. van Dreesen would kick against it, so why say anything at all?"

Sheriff Engle's nod was a little less sheepish than Roland was expecting. "I barely got the chance to say anything at all. Her lawyers all but ran our people off the scene, so we—what was it they said, now?—so we 'wouldn't compromise any further investigations by more qualified personnel.' That would be you, I guess."

"Lucky me."

They turned left onto a winding dirt road that climbed gently past a couple of small farms before plunging again into the woods. Every few hundred yards, a driveway led off to the right, marked by a stone pillar carved with a name. They passed by Lakeview, Trout Bank, and Sempel's Landing.

"All right," Roland said at last, "let me see if I've got this straight. The house looks like a howitzer shell hit it. You don't know why, and Mrs. van Dreesen didn't encourage you to look very hard, so you didn't. There's no gas that anyone knows of, and the hot water boiler was far too small to blow up with that much force. So unless the house was bombed by a Zeppelin you haven't told me about, there's just one thing left: bootleggers."

"It's possible, I guess." The sheriff volunteered nothing further.

"All right," said Roland, "you're going to make me work for it, so I'll ask: do you have any bootlegger trouble in Arkham?"

"Did you ever hear of a mug named Johnny V?"

"I've been down south for a while, remember? Who is this Johnny V? Is he local talent?"

"Boston. Real bad news, from what they say."

"And what brought him to little old Arkham? I'm guessing he's not a music lover?"

"Word is, he's been expanding up the coast over the last few months, but there's a local guy who's been holding out."

"Go on."

"Now, this orchestra wasn't exactly the Metropolitan Opera."

"I got that impression. So their quest for booze put them in between these two bootleggers, and someone was a sore loser?"

"It crossed my mind." Sheriff Engle frogged his mouth. "But I can't prove it."

"Did you even try?" Roland asked. "Or are you in with one of these bootleggers? The local boy, at a guess."

The sheriff let out a snort of laughter. "Sure. That's why I'm telling a G-man about him."

"You left out his name."

"Leo De Luca. Happy?"

"So, how come he's still walking around?"

Sheriff Engle spread his hands. "No evidence, no witnesses. There's never been much booze in Arkham, outside of the college. New England Congregationalists, you see."

"I get the picture," Roland said wearily. People almost never gave up their local bootleggers: out of loyalty, out of fear, or from simple distrust of the Feds, they kept silent. "So did this local boy De Luca blow up the orchestra, or did the Boston outfit do it?"

Sheriff Engle grimaced briefly. "You're the expert," he said. "I just lock up drunks and chase burglars. Anyway, this is it."

The entrance to Pine Beach was marked by two rustic-looking stone pillars, joined by a wrought-iron arch with the name in old-fashioned scrollwork. They bumped down the rutted driveway for another quarter of a mile before the sheriff brought the car to a halt. Roland sat for a moment, taking in the scene.

The trees bowed away from the house, as though some giant had pushed them askew. At the center of the clearing, nothing stood higher than a couple of feet. A crumbling chimney loomed over a jumble of wood and rubble.

"Keep going," the sheriff said with a dark laugh. Roland walked up the path, past what remained of the walls, and took a deep breath.

On the far side of the house, almost nothing remained but hints of the stone foundations. A halo of rubble ringed the scene: shattered timbers and fragments of masonry radiated out from the ruins like the rays on a child's drawing of the sun.

In 1918, Roland had marched through Château-Thierry with

Pershing, during the Second Battle of the Marne. The little village had been blown apart by German and Allied artillery in the war's last gasp, but Pine Beach was in even worse shape. The far side of the house looked shorn off rather than blown up: it was reduced to a couple of courses of stone, surrounded by a wide ring of debris.

Boot prints and tire tracks on the muddy ground reminded him that the scene was far from pristine. He turned to Sheriff Engle. "Where were the bodies?"

The sheriff stretched out his arms in an all-encompassing gesture. "All over," he said. "A few were whole, some were in pieces, some were…"

"Some were what?"

"Hard to describe. Crushed, I guess. Like a bug when you step on it and drag your shoe."

"Where were they taken?"

"The morgue at St. Mary's Hospital, first. The last one went back to his family two days ago."

"Autopsies?"

"No. Cause of death was pretty clear."

Roland looked around him and was forced to concede that this was true. "Any identification problems?"

The sheriff shrugged. "You'd have to ask the coroner. All I know is, the numbers tallied. Thirty-eight in the orchestra, including the composer. Thirty-eight in the rubble."

Roland wrote this down. They skirted the foundation in silence. Roland paused to examine a fallen roof beam. Once a pine trunk as thick as a beer barrel, it was shredded like a chewed toothpick. He turned and followed the line of the fallen timber back to the house.

"Looking for something?" asked Sheriff Engle.

"Everything on this side is pointing out from the site of the explosion," said Roland. "Find the middle and we find the origin."

Roland stepped into the foundation and stopped dead. In contrast to the outside of the house, the wreckage within the building's original footprint was a chaotic jumble, without pattern or order. He walked around for a while, trying to make sense of it, but it seemed increasingly that there was no sense to be made.

"Scratch that plan," he said at last. "I never saw dynamite do that before. How about you?"

The sheriff shrugged. "I've never seen dynamite do anything before."

"The joys of a quiet life," Roland said sourly.

Roland walked around the perimeter of the foundation. The house had been a big one, all right. He had seen smaller castles. Roland widened his path, spiraling outward in the hope of finding something—anything—that might tell him more.

The fountain he had seen in the old photograph was shorn off at the same level as the foundation: ankle height on one of the nymphs. The rest of the marble was nowhere to be seen. Something about the stone caught Roland's eye.

"Sheriff Engle!" The sheriff came trotting over. "Take a look at this." Roland indicated the stump of the fountain.

"You found something?" The sheriff looked where Roland was pointing. "Huh." Sheriff Engle straightened up and pushed his hat back a little.

Despite the evident violence of the explosion, the stone was not shattered. Instead, the top of the stump was smooth, like freshly cut cheese.

"Looks like someone sawed it off," Sheriff Engle said at last.

"That's a good way to put it," said Roland. "Could our merry pranksters have done that, do you think?"

"If they had a quarry saw, maybe," said Sheriff Engle. "My pa worked with granite over in Quincy," he explained in response to Roland's questioning look. "They had one—water powered. It was big, however, and very slow, and it was set up for vertical cuts. Something like this, now…it would take some doing."

Roland straightened up and strode back to the remains of the house. By the time the sheriff caught up with him, he had cleared an area about three feet square. The stone here was darker, a local granite rather than imported marble, but the signs were the same. The top of each stone looked as though it had been sliced off with a hot knife. Roland raised an eyebrow at Sheriff Engle, who shook his head slowly.

"I never saw the like," he said. "And this was done right here, not at any quarry. See how level it is from one stone to the next? No one can lay a foundation that regular."

"Something else is off, too," Roland said. "Have you seen any sign of burning anywhere?"

"Burning?"

"Yes. An explosion's nothing more than a very fast, very intense fire. There should be some charring, especially around the heart of the explosion."

"Huh." The sheriff looked mystified. "That makes sense, now you come to mention it. I didn't see a trace of a fire anywhere. Does that rule out dynamite?"

"I don't know. Between that and the stone, though, it bothers me. Did you say Arkham's a college town?"

"Miskatonic," said the sheriff. "Almost as old as Harvard and Yale." A hint of local pride crept into his voice.

"Good," said Roland. "Maybe a geologist or a chemist can make sense of this. It's got to add up somehow. You said the noise was heard a long way off?"

Sheriff Engle nodded. "Heard—and felt, too. A picture fell off the wall in my office."

"Like an earthquake?"

"Hard to say. I never felt an earthquake before."

"All right. What about the sound? Did it sound like an explosion?"

"Just a rumble by the time it reached town. Something like thunder, maybe. One of the witnesses said it sounded like a locomotive crash—but she was close enough to hear the debris falling."

Roland turned on Sheriff Engle. "What witness?" he almost yelled. "When were you planning to tell me there was a witness?"

"Not an eyewitness," the sheriff rebutted, "just someone who heard the noise. Name's Talbot, Miss Talbot. She was here with the orchestra—took the photos in the file."

"I remember. From New York? There was an address on the back of the photographs."

"Right. She went back soon after."

"I'll need to talk to her."

Leaving the sheriff still examining the edge of the foundation, Roland returned to his spiral path. Beyond the fountain the lawn narrowed slightly, leaving an avenue of trees framing the way to the lake. Their trunks were bizarrely studded with debris, reminding Roland of photographs he had seen of tornado damage in Kansas. A piece of metal silverware jutted from one tree, pushed in hilt-deep as if the tree were a baked potato. Lower down, something that might have been a table leg jutted out to one side.

Roland turned to look out across the lake. A single cabin was visible on the opposite shore, crowded by trees and much less grand than the Worthington House had been. If Roland ignored the devastation behind him, the place was peaceful and idyllic. A gentle breeze stirred the trees and carried the sound of lapping water to his ears. The only other sound was the crunch of Sheriff Engle's boots as he approached.

"Seen enough?" he asked.

Roland held up a hand for silence. "Do you hear that?" he said. Sheriff Engle stood and listened.

The sound was far off, almost too soft to hear.

"What is that?" Roland asked. "A bird?"

The sheriff listened for a moment longer. "Not any bird I know," he said at last. "Mostly you'll hear loons and woodpeckers around here, maybe a hawk once in a while, some smaller birds."

"I haven't heard a thing since we got here," said Roland.

"Me neither," said Sheriff Engle. "Not even a squirrel."

The wind shifted and the sound became clearer. Thin and monotonous, there was nothing musical about it. The image of a suspended bamboo pipe sprang into Roland's mind, with a ceaseless prairie wind blowing across one end. It was the sound a movie-house musician might conjure up to accompany a blurred and silent newsreel image from out West, of rolling tumbleweeds and abandoned shacks half-buried by drifting sand. For no reason he could fathom, Roland suddenly felt bitterly cold and desperately lonely.

The wind shifted again, tearing the monotonous piping into shreds and breaking the spell that had kept the two men rooted to the spot in silence. They looked at each other briefly, each moved by a sudden need to know that the sound had affected the other in the same way, but broke eye contact immediately. By an unspoken mutual agreement they turned and walked back toward the house.

It was a few minutes before Roland felt able to speak. At last he set his shoulders, swept the scene with an overly deliberate gaze, and said, "I got what I need for now. Let's head back." Sheriff Engle nodded silently and they walked back toward the car.

The sound remained in Roland's head, even though he knew

his ears could no longer hear it. He looked back at the ruins and shivered: it was as though he saw them—truly saw them—for the first time. The devastation of Château-Thierry suddenly seemed like a ridiculous comparison, its destruction by heavy artillery altogether too benign an analogy. Dynamite was far kinder, somehow, than whatever had happened here.

Roland's mind kept turning unbidden to fragments of the Bible: Sodom and Gomorrah, the Book of Revelation, and pillars of fire from the heavens. He fought a rising sense of panic, and he had to check his pace to keep from running. He forced himself into a heavy marching pace, taking comfort in the automatic, unthinking motion and holding tight to his memories of the Marne like a child clutches a teddy bear in the dark.

Minutes or hours later, the two men reached the sheriff's car and climbed in without a word. The inexplicable fear lifted as they drove back to the road, but neither man spoke until they were back in Arkham. They parted with few words, Roland agreeing to keep Sheriff Engle informed of his progress.

Chapter 4

"Welcome back, hon! We missed you at breakfast!"

Roland was relying on the banal cheer of the diner to clear the last of the strange mood that had overtaken him by the lake. Two different cops sat at the counter, giving him the same look their brothers in blue had the previous day. Roland ignored them and chose a table at the back.

Velma's smile faltered just a hair as she took his order—only a trained observer would have noticed, but Roland could tell she had seen something in his face. What had happened out there? How could a half-heard sound shake a grown man so badly? Roland had faced German machine guns and bootleggers' Thompsons, but the only feeling that came close to his experience at Pine Beach was the sudden clutch of panic that had followed the alarm of a mustard-gas attack. He needed to think of something else.

Roland gulped his coffee and pulled out his notebook. An explosion remained the most likely explanation, despite the lack of burning and the strange appearance of the shorn-off stones. He would go to the local college and look for a geologist who could explain it. He also needed to look into Sheriff Engle's bootleg war: he cursed himself briefly for forgetting to ask the sheriff where the local boy—he flipped to the right page—Leo De Luca could be found. He would also see if the Bureau had anything on De Luca, or on Johnny V, the pride of Boston.

"What's the word?" The waitress arrived with Roland's food and began eyeing his notebook. He flipped the book closed.

"Right now," he said, with his most charming smile, "the word is lunch." He began to eat, ignoring the fact that she stood there just a second too long. He had nothing to tell, not even if it were Hoover himself who was asking.

Roland felt a little calmer by the time he left the diner. He had one line of inquiry to pursue, and that was enough for now. He looked into the police station, but was told that Sheriff Engle had been called to the countryside and no one knew when he might be back. Roland suspected that the sheriff might be taking a little fishing trip about now; Roland himself was certainly looking forward to putting more distance between himself and Pine Beach just as soon as he could.

It came as no surprise that no one in the station would admit that they had ever heard of Leo De Luca. Judging by the strawberry noses on a couple of the older bulls, Roland was probably asking some of the bootlegger's regular customers. Johnny V's name was a little more familiar, or so it seemed. His surname was Valone, Roland learned, and yes, he was from Boston or thereabouts, according to a couple of officers, who had heard it from a distant cousin or passing acquaintance in the city. As for Arkham, Roland was told quite firmly that Arkham did not have a bootlegging problem; Sheriff Engle's comment about New England Congregationalists was repeated almost word for word.

Roland would have to find some other way to track down these two entrepreneurs. Perhaps the Boston Field Office had files on Johnny Valone and Leo De Luca. It was worth a cable to find out.

On his way to the telegraph office, Roland noticed the jazz club again. It was just as obvious as it had been the day before: the very first place anyone would think to look if they wanted illicit booze or the people who moved it, and therefore the very last place that was likely to have any connection with bootlegging. On the other hand, he might have overestimated the worthy constables of Arkham. It could be that they were dumb enough, or confident enough, to let the place move hooch under their noses. It would not be the first time he had seen one place allowed to remain open so that the cops had somewhere to make a show if they needed to—or somewhere to drink if they wanted to.

This early in the day, of course, the place was closed up tight. Roland resolved to come back in the evening and see what he could find out. For now he would send his cable, go back to the hotel to clean up, and then see if he could scare up a geologist at this famous college. His stomach knotted at the thought of going back to Pine Beach, but next time he would have a scientist with him, to give him a safe and boring explanation for everything that was so strange and disturbing about the scene.

It was just after two when he returned to the hotel. He was three paces across the lobby when a woman's voice stopped him.

"Are you the federal man here about Pine Beach?"

Roland's heart stopped as dead as the rest of him. The last thing he needed was Mrs. van Dreesen dropping by to check on his progress. When he turned around, though, the woman who had just risen from one of the threadbare armchairs was anything but a toffee-nosed Knickerbocker. A Louise Brooks bob framed a pair of smoky eyes that held Roland's gaze with disarming frankness and obvious intelligence—and something else that Roland could not quite identify, hidden down deep. She wore country tweeds rather than flapper beads, but she was the type who would look good in silk or sackcloth. Roland cleared his throat.

"Who's asking?"

The young woman pulled a business card out of a jacket pocket.

"Edie Talbot. I photographed the scene. Also—," she hesitated for a fraction of a second, "—I knew Oliver Haldane. I was here to write a profile and report on the new piece for *The Music Trades.*"

"The what?"

"*The Music Trades*. It's a magazine from New York."

Roland nodded, remembering the New York address from the back of the photographs.

"Thank you for finding me, Miss Talbot. Or is it…?"

"It's Miss." Her tone was professional rather than flirtatious, but not unfriendly.

"Agent Roland Banks, Bureau of Investigation." Roland flashed his badge. "Have you been in Arkham since it happened?"

"No. I—I went back to New York right afterward. Somehow I just couldn't stay on there. I came back when I heard you were in town."

"I'm glad you did, Miss Talbot," said Roland, "and I certainly want to hear what you have to say, but it happens that right now I have to go. Where can I reach you, say, tomorrow morning?"

She looked disappointed, but not offended. "Here. I can…"

"Wait a minute." The first of Edie's photographs had shown no one else on the scene, and she had just implied that she was either staying at Pine Beach or somewhere very close by. Sheriff Engle had said she was a witness, after all. The college could wait: those stones would not be going anywhere. He motioned Edie back to her chair and seated himself across from her.

"I'm sorry, Miss Talbot," he said, "I was a little slow on the draw there. Am I right in thinking you were near the house when it happened?"

"About a quarter mile away. My editor knows someone who knows the Sempels."

"Sempel's Landing? I passed by it this morning."

"That's right. When it happened I ran out to try and help, but there was so clearly nothing to be done. I telephoned the police, photographed everything I could, met with them when they arrived, and then left to develop the film. It was little enough, but it was all I could think of to do."

"It was plenty, Miss Talbot, and good thinking. Most people would have lost their heads in those circumstances."

"I would have lost mine, I think, if I hadn't had the photography to occupy it." There was the faintest tremble in her voice. "I've never seen anything like it." Roland could think of no answer.

"I haven't explored Arkham yet," he said at last, "so I'm unsure where would be a good place for us to talk in private. Do you have any suggestions?"

"Not the police station?" Edie sounded surprised, but Roland shook his head.

"I'd prefer not," he said. "It might surprise you, but the local law doesn't always welcome us federal types with open arms. The only other places I know are the diner—"

"Privacy isn't exactly Velma's long suit," Edie put in, with a mischievous smile.

"I'd noticed. We could stay here, I suppose, but…" He tilted his head subtly toward the front desk and the open door behind it.

"I understand," she said. "How about the tea room at the station? Plenty of noise and bustle there."

Fifteen minutes later, they were seated at a lace-covered table sharing coffee and cake at the train station. After bringing their order, the waitress ignored them as thoroughly as the handful of fellow patrons did. Roland brought out his notebook and uncapped his pen, writing Edie's name at the top of a fresh page.

"All right, Miss Talbot," he said, "in your own words, tell me everything you saw and heard." Edie's face fell a little, but she steeled herself and started talking.

"It was around dusk," she began. "I was inside writing up my notes from the day's rehearsals. I could just hear the music coming across from Pine Beach. It was a hot day, and they would often work with the windows open." She waited for Roland to stop writing, and continued at his nod.

"It was a section I hadn't heard before—the choral passage from the inscription."

"Inscription?"

"Something Oliver had found in a museum. I've got the particulars in my notes if it's important."

"Probably not. Then what happened?"

"Everything shook—just how I imagine an earthquake would be. The sound was…" she struggled, clearly searching for the right words, and then shook her head in frustration. "I think it went dark, just for a second. Then it was still again, with just the sound of falling debris. I ran across as fast as I could, but it was all over. I'm sure the other witness could tell you more."

Roland's head snapped up. "The other witness?"

"Yes—surely you know about him already?"

"I wish I did. Who is he?"

"A strange little local man. I think he has a shack in the woods somewhere. At any rate, the boys would buy moonshine from him and make fun behind his back. He's odd, as I said: the drink's gotten to him, I think. What is his name?" Her brow wrinkled in thought. "Ellis, Elmer, Elwood—El-something, at any rate."

"You saw him there after the…explosion?"

"He was kneeling at the edge of the woods. He looked up at me and just started screaming." She closed her eyes briefly. "A horrible sound it was, truly horrible. When the police came he grabbed one of them by the jacket and started babbling nonsense at him, something about the sky cracking open and the world ending." She sighed. "Poor man. The shock was too much for him. It nearly was for me, too."

Roland wrote furiously. This Ellis, or whatever his name was, sounded like the first viable suspect Roland had come across. He had known backwoods moonshiners to be vicious and resourceful, if a little reckless and apt to lose control of their chemistry. A scenario sprang into his mind, fully formed: an overheard slight, attempted arson, something going wrong, shock and remorse tipping an already rocky mind over the edge—it made an appealing amount of sense. But what could have gone so catastrophically wrong as to level half of the house to its foundation? Whatever had happened, the moonshiner was Roland's best—and possibly only—chance to find out. "Do you know what happened to him?"

"They took him away," Edie said. "The police did. He was ranting and raving, trying to get someone to listen to him. They wanted us both out of the way so they could examine the—the damage. I went to develop my photographs, but he refused to leave. It took three of them to wrestle him to the ground. They threw him in the back of a car and drove him away."

Roland finished writing and looked up. Edie's face was pale, her eyes large. It had cost her something to remember it.

"I'll be sure to ask the sheriff's office about that," Roland said, slashing a savage underline into his notebook. "Now, you say you were working on an article about this new musical work?"

"Yes—*Rites of Apsu.*"

"That's a strange name."

"It's Mesopotamian. Or Babylonian, or something. I don't know the difference, to be honest."

"From the museum piece you mentioned?"

"That's right. It was on display at the Met when Oliver saw it."

"And you came to Arkham at the same time as the orchestra?"

"The same day, at any rate."

"And you've been with them every day?"

"Most of the time, I'd say, but not all. Are you going to ask me if they had any enemies?"

Roland looked up and saw a gleam of amusement in her smoky eyes. "That was going to be one of my questions, although accident hasn't been ruled out yet. But let's start with enemies. I've heard they didn't exactly make themselves popular with the neighbors."

"The business with the motorboat?"

"Among other things. And not just here. I read that Oliver Haldane was a controversial type."

"He liked to play the *enfant terrible.* A lot of artists do."

"Can you elaborate?"

"Well, his *Missa Negra* was condemned from the pulpit because Oliver used a choral section based on a witch's spell book from Salem. He liked the Mesopotamian carving because it came from a cursed city. He always said that it was the responsibility of the true artist to challenge mediocrity by breaking down the conventions of society to free the human spirit from the shackles of civilization. People have called him a Communist, an anarchist, a Satanist—he loves notoriety." She took a brief, shaky pause. "Loved, I mean."

"I see," said Roland. Spiritualism had flourished like a weed after the destruction of the Great War, and the fashionable wasters of the art world saw black magic as a way to seem dangerous and interesting.

"Was there anyone, or any group, in particular who was so outraged that they could have tried to kill him, or his orchestra?"

"No one in particular, no."

"I've heard that bootleggers are active in the area," said Roland. "Based on what I've heard about the orchestra, it seems possible that they somehow found themselves caught between two rival gangs. You already told me that they did business with someone named Ellis, or Elmer, or Elwood, or something similar. Do you know of any other criminal contacts?"

Edie was silent for a moment. Roland waited.

"I don't know of anyone else in these parts," she said at last.

"Does the name Leo De Luca mean anything to you? Or Johnny Valone, also known as Johnny V?" She shook her head.

"Miss Talbot," he said, "Thank you for your help. If there's anything else you remember—anything at all…"

"I'll leave you a message at the hotel," she promised.

Chapter 5

"The sheriff's still out of town." The desk sergeant did not even bother to look up at Roland this time.

"I'm not looking for the sheriff," Roland said. Sheriff Engle had neglected to mention the old moonshiner earlier; there was no telling what else he might have held back—what else the other cops might let slip if Roland pushed them.

"I need to talk to every one of your people who went out to Pine Beach that day." He said. "Everyone who saw or spoke to the witness—the one that the sheriff forgot to tell me about." He slapped his growing stack of files down on the counter and lowered his voice to a growl. "Right now."

That made the sergeant look up. The two men locked stares for a long moment, but Roland was used to these territorial battles with local law enforcement. The sergeant broke off first.

"You'll need to ask the captain," he said, clearly trying to sound more confident than he felt. "But he's—" Roland was already striding through the wicket to the bullpen.

"Thanks," he said over his shoulder as he headed for a door with "Captain" in gold letters on its frosted-glass window. Two minutes later he was back on the street, having learned that the old moonshiner's name was Elmer White and that he had been taken to the Arkham Sanatorium.

Storming the local police station like an enemy trench was far from standard procedure. Roland was supposed to show up, flash his badge, and invoke the might of the Bureau of Investigation, whereupon the locals were supposed to tug their forelocks and give him whatever he asked for. Standard procedure had clearly been designed by someone who had never left headquarters, but Roland had always gone by the book despite the book's obvious problems. He told himself he was planting the Bureau's flag on the moral high ground, but in hindsight, perhaps he had just been covering his rear, toeing the line so no black mark could ever sully his file. A lot of good that had done him in Jubal County, and he would be damned if he'd let another bunch of local hicks make a fool of him.

The momentum of his anger and frustration carried Roland into the asylum like an express train. With the prospect of an eyewitness hanging before him like a vision of the Holy Grail, the qualms Roland had felt at the sight of the place the previous day evaporated. Roland had become an irresistible force, and heaven help anyone who tried to play the immovable object.

"Bureau of Investigation." He shoved his badge in the face of a startled receptionist. "Agent Roland Banks. I need to see one of your patients: the name is White comma Elmer. Right now."

"Visiting hours are…" The receptionist was made of sterner stuff than the police captain. Perhaps working around asylum inmates gave a person confidence. But Roland was not about to be stalled.

"Never mind visiting hours," he snapped. "This is federal business. Elmer White—where is he?"

"I'm sorry, but…"

"Don't be sorry; be cooperative. Five minutes from now, either I'll be looking at Elmer White or I'll be hauling you off in cuffs for obstructing a federal investigation. The choice is yours." He made a show of looking at his watch as the receptionist reached for her phone. Throwing his weight around was more of a thrill than he expected, and he could see how some agents got to liking it a little too much. *Watch yourself*, he thought. *You're a lawman, not a bully.* But he could not deny that it felt good.

A nurse marched up to the desk, wearing a crisply starched uniform and an even starchier expression. She opened her mouth to speak, but Roland struck first.

"Thank you for your cooperation." His badge was already in his hand. "Agent Roland Banks, Bureau of Investigation, to see your patient Elmer White without delay. Federal business." He pushed past her and set off down the corridor.

"What's the room number?" he shot over one shoulder as the nurse trailed in his wake. He kept talking, giving her no opportunity to protest. "I'll have some questions for you, too. You'd better bring his patient file." He turned a corner to find a heavy door blocked by two burly orderlies in hospital whites. They stood with folded arms like a pair of granite statues, and they looked about as easy to move. Roland was forced to stop walking.

"If I call your superiors," the nurse's voice was cold, "will I hear the same story you just told poor Miss Millicent? Stand aside or face arrest for obstruction?" Roland bit back an ungentlemanly response.

"Nurse…" he began, turning to face her.

"Heather."

"Nurse Heather," he said, trying not to lose his momentum, "what you will hear is that a house was destroyed, thirty-eight lives lost, and that Elmer White is definitely a witness and quite possibly a suspect. You will also hear that Elmer White is suspected of multiple violations of the Volstead Act and that these violations will be reported to the Bureau of Internal Revenue's Prohibition Unit, which will probably begin its own proceedings against Mr. White. I am a federal agent engaged in a federal investigation, and any lack of cooperation on your part will be reported and may result in criminal proceedings for obstruction. Do I make myself clear?"

To Roland's annoyance, Nurse Heather did not look at all intimidated. On the contrary, she looked a little amused.

"Abundantly clear, Agent Banks," she said. "And now, let me make myself abundantly clear in my turn."

Roland raised an eyebrow to let her know she had his attention. He wished those two toughs were not right behind him, and he knew Nurse Heather could see him wishing it.

"In the first place," she said, with a hint of a malicious smile, "anyone who comes in here ranting and bullying and claiming to be above the rules is exhibiting the classic symptoms of paranoid schizophrenia with delusions of grandeur. It is my duty to have any such person restrained until a formal diagnosis can be obtained. In plain English, if you come in here acting crazy I can lock you up until Dr. Mintz has time to examine you. And," her mouth twitched up at one corner, "I'm the one who decides what 'acting crazy' looks like. So unless you'd like to spend tonight in a padded room and most of tomorrow trying to prove you're sane, why don't you ease up on the gas? Okay?"

She was a smug one, all right, and Roland had no doubt she could make good on her threat. Heck, she could probably shoot him full of something and actually make him crazy, and then he would be here for good. Given how things had gone in Virginia, the Bureau might not even try to get him back. Roland found his jaw was clenched too tight for talking, so he answered her with a shrug and a spread of the hands.

"All right, then," she said, turning on her heel. "For one thing, you're heading the wrong way. Follow me." Roland knew that he must have felt more foolish at some point in his life, but right at that moment he could not call the occasion to mind.

Nurse Heather kept talking as they walked, probably to keep the upper hand as Roland had tried to do earlier. The two orderlies followed, just a little too close so that Roland felt on edge. No doubt that was on purpose as well.

"Did you ever hear the saying, 'a lunatic has the strength of ten'?" she asked, clearly not expecting an answer. "Well, I can tell you it's true. That's why we like to keep our patients nice and calm, and that means that we don't like raised voices or other displays of aggression. It stirs them up, and before you know it, you can have a riot on your hands. And in a place like this, it's nothing like a standard prison riot. It's more like a painting by Hieronymus Bosch. Ever seen his work? Never mind. The point is, don't go bulling around, because it gets the patients excited and that makes problems for everyone. I'd tell J. Edgar Hoover or President Coolidge the same thing, and I'd lock them up just as fast if they didn't listen." She turned her head to look Roland in the eye. "Don't test me on that.

"So—Elmer White," she continued without skipping a beat.

"Brought in by the Arkham police on the day the house was destroyed. They said they found him there in a highly agitated state. He wouldn't or couldn't answer their questions, wasn't making sense, and became aggressive. They brought him here in handcuffs, upset and incoherent. He seemed to think the world was ending, or had ended when the house was destroyed. Dr. Mintz diagnosed paranoid schizophrenia—remember I mentioned that?—complicated by brain and liver damage from a lifetime of alcohol addiction. He prescribed morphine to keep the patient docile pending a decision on long-term treatment. There's no next of kin that anyone knows of, so the decision will rest with the county."

"How docile?" Roland asked. If Elmer was drugged up to the eyebrows, he would not be much use as a witness, and who knew how long it might take to bring him back.

"See for yourself," said Nurse Heather, unlocking a door to the right and motioning Roland inside.

The first thing that struck Roland was the smell. A nauseating mixture of organic waste, decay, and suppuration assaulted his nostrils, overlaid but not overshadowed by bleach and sharper chemical smells. Surely it could not all be coming from one person. At least none of the stains on the mattress and sheet looked very fresh.

A small, scabby man was strapped to the bed. Roland put his age at about seventy. His slack face was turned to the wall, but it was clear that his eyes saw nothing. Apart from the bed and its occupant, the room was completely empty. There was not even a chair to sit in.

At a gesture from Nurse Heather, one of the massive orderlies muscled in behind Roland. "Cole will stay with you," she said, "for your own safety." Roland looked down at the shrunken, wizened figure strapped to the mattress.

"My safety?" Roland said. "From him?"

"You'd be surprised," said the nurse. "Schizophrenics are like nitroglycerin: one little nudge and they blow up. I saw a patient smaller than this one break out of restraints in less than ten seconds. The bed frame was bent like a banana. And you're here to ask about the house, which can't fail to get him agitated." She flashed Roland a bitter smile and left.

Roland leaned over the bed as Cole settled his impassive bulk across the doorway.

"Best not to get too close." The orderly's voice was surprisingly soft. "They can move fast when they turn: grab your tie or rip your ear off before you know it." Despite himself, Roland glanced down at the thick leather straps that held the patient's wrists to the bed frame. They looked reassuringly sturdy.

"Elmer White?" he asked, as gently as he could manage. The old man gave no acknowledgment.

"Elmer?" Roland repeated. "Can you hear me?" Still nothing. He might as well be talking to a sack of potatoes.

"Mr. White." He let an official edge into his voice. "My name is Agent Roland Banks, and I'm with the Bureau of Investigation." An eyelid flickered. Roland decided to treat it as a good sign. He would start with some innocuous questions and see how things went.

"Have you ever done business with Leo De Luca?" Elmer's eyes slid away from the nothing they had been looking at and fastened onto the blank wall. His stillness changed almost imperceptibly, becoming a little more deliberate.

"How about Johnny Valone? Have you ever heard that name before?" White said nothing.

This tack was getting him nowhere. Roland tried a lighter tone. "Tell me, Elmer," he said, "how do you like it here? Cole here, he seems like a real swell guy. I bet you two talk and laugh all the time. That Nurse Heather, too—boy, what a peach! Does she tuck you in just right, make sure those straps are good and snug?" Roland sensed, rather than saw, that his words were getting through the blanket of morphine that enveloped the old moonshiner. Although Elmer had not moved perceptibly, the rising tension in him was palpable.

"And how's Dr. Mintz?" Roland asked. "I haven't met him yet, but he sounds like a real smart man. How's he treating you? Do you lie on a couch and talk about your mother? Take cold, refreshing baths? Or is he one of those modern types, with big electrical machines to fix you up?" One of Elmer's hands twitched in its leather restraint: that last question had struck a nerve.

"Yes, I bet he is, Elmer," Roland went on, maintaining his conversational tone. "I bet you're having a whale of a time and getting the most modern treatments. Why, I bet you're having just as much fun as a Vanderbilt princess taking the rest cure in Switzerland. Well, I have good news for you, Elmer. All you have to do is keep stonewalling me and you get to stay here forever. You and Dr. Mintz can whoop it up from dawn to dusk, and no one will try to stop either of you. Not unless one of your relatives steps in and stops the party. Do you have a big family, Elmer? Anyone likely to come and get you?"

Elmer's eyes were moving now, sliding foggily from side to side like those of a hunted animal. Roland pressed his advantage.

"That's what I figured, Elmer. Nurse Heather tells me no one's been asking about you—no family, no friends, no one at all. Leo De Luca hasn't come to call. I don't see any flowers with love from Johnny Valone. Not even a bunch of grapes. Well, I guess they don't want to disturb you when you're having such a good time with your new pal, Dr. Mintz." Another twitch. Roland had no idea what Mintz had been doing to the old rummy, but he was willing to bet it was more than just the morphine sedation Nurse Heather had mentioned.

"Leo..." The voice was paper-thin, but it was there.

"He's not coming, Elmer. I'm your only way out of here. I know it, and you know it, too. So what do you say? Just a few little questions?"

"Leo..." It took some effort, but Elmer fixed Roland with one rheumy eye. "Leo'n'me...got...business."

Roland smiled, deliberately showing his teeth. "There—that wasn't so hard, Elmer, was it now? And you know what? I'm a good scout, so I'm not even going to ask you what kind of business. No sir, I'll just mind my own beeswax on that score. But the thing is, Elmer, I'd really like to talk to your buddy Leo. I hear Johnny V's giving him some trouble, and I want to help Leo out." The bleary eye did not move.

"I get it, Elmer," Roland went on. "You don't trust me because I'm a G-man. But here's the straight dope: I'm not here for you, and I'm not here for Leo. You two can peddle your giggle water all over Arkham and across three counties for all I care. No sir, it's Johnny V I'm after. He's the big fish that's going to get me a promotion and a fat pay raise. And after I fix Johnny's wagon, I'll be far, far away in Washington, smoking cigars with J. Edgar Hoover and telling him how we can pinch a certain Mr. Capone. Little old Arkham won't ever cross my mind again. So you see, we all come up aces—you, me, and Leo."

Roland gave this a moment to sink in. The morphine was not making Elmer's mind any faster, he knew, but he hoped his breezy tone would smooth out any bumps. Elmer's other eye finally caught up with the first one, looking right at him.

"But there's just one little problem, Elmer," he said. "You can see what it is, can't you? I have to talk to Leo so I can clue him in on the plan. Otherwise it's all for nothing. So be a pal, Elmer, and tell me where I can find him."

After all that talking, it was a kind of agony for Roland to wait for Elmer's answer. The old rummy was trying, he could tell, fighting through the haze of morphine, but it held him almost as securely as the leather straps.

"Leo…"

"Yes?"

"Th…th'Night'ngale." Elmer's voice was getting stronger, although it was still no more than a whisper.

"Well, all right, Elmer," Roland said. "You've done your part and I'll do mine. I'll talk to Leo and get everything set up. Then we'll bust you out of here and we'll all three go fix Johnny V together." He gave the old man a comforting pat on the shoulder. "In fact, I'm going to take care of the paperwork right now."

Roland rose as if to leave, taking a step toward the door before he asked his real question.

"Say, Elmer," he said, "just to double check—it was Johnny V who blew up that big house by the lake, wasn't it? Must've taken a mess of dynamite."

Elmer was very still for a moment, and Roland started to worry that he had lost him to the morphine again. Then the old man's mouth opened wider than the gates of hell and a sound came out like a thousand cats being neutered with dull knives. The bed rocked as Elmer thrashed against his restraints.

"The sky!" Elmer's voice was suddenly as clear as a Baptist preacher's. "It tore through! Licked it up! Licked it all up!" Roland felt himself picked up like a Kewpie doll. Before he could react, he was outside the room and Cole was locking the door. Elmer's voice was muffled, but Roland could pick out a word here and there: "eyes," "tongue," "teeth," "sky," "flute," "balloon," and others, apparently at random.

"Shouldn't have gotten him excited," the big man said in his oddly gentle voice. "Got to get the doctor now. You got to leave." Roland thought for a moment that Cole expected him to comply without argument, but then he realized that it made no difference to the orderly whether he resisted or not. He decided to go quietly.

"Was that how he was when he came in?" he asked.

Cole nodded gravely.

Neither one spoke the rest of the way outside, and Roland felt a little relieved that he did not encounter Nurse Heather as he left.

Chapter 6

Outside the asylum, the air felt cooler. Roland took a few deep breaths and reviewed his options. It had been a Bearcat of a day, and he was not proud of some of the things he had done, but he had a few pieces of information to show for it. He had crossed some lines, but he felt far less guilty than he would have expected. He strolled across to the square, collecting his thoughts as he went.

Whatever had wiped out that mansion, it had been big. Dynamite was the most likely explanation, even though the scene did not look quite right. It certainly made more sense than a tongue full of teeth reaching down from a hole in the sky.

The bootlegger war felt like a pretty solid angle, although Roland was not sure yet how it all fit together. It seemed most likely that somebody had blown up somebody else's customers. This Leo De Luca could probably clear up the details.

Roland would need some kind of leverage, of course. The threat of a raid, or the promise of protection from Johnny V or from the Prohibition Unit, would only work if Leo was gullible enough to trust the word of a G-man, and Leo was probably not that naïve. It had only worked on Elmer because the old coot was so befuddled by the doctor's morphine and his own coffin varnish.

Roland needed to know more about both Leo De Luca and Johnny V. It seemed like days, rather than hours, since he had cabled Boston for their Bureau files, but it would be tomorrow at the earliest before he heard anything back. Right now, he could pass either one of them in the street and not know it.

As tired as Roland felt, he was not ready to call it a day and go back to the hotel. He would only end up beating his head against those files again, and there was nothing more to be gained there. He had not yet burned off all of the frustration and anger that had propelled him into the asylum like a wrecking ball. He needed to unwind somehow.

That was when he decided to visit the Nightingale Club. The sun had set while Roland was in the asylum, and the place was probably open for business. Maybe he would go inside and see if Leo De Luca was in there, as Elmer had told him he would be. Maybe he would have a drink to settle his mind down. It was the sixth year of Prohibition and his fourth as a federal agent, but despite this—or perhaps because of it—the thought of whiskey gave him the same illicit thrill as his first schoolyard glimpse of a French postcard.

There was always the risk that Roland might run into one of the Arkham cops or some other bigwig in the gin mill. It was not unknown for federal agents to arrest a local police chief or even a mayor in a speakeasy, and Roland had been the kind of agent who relished these collars in particular. If the Bureau were to hear of any transgression on his part, far too many people would be far too happy to have something on the Boy Scout.

On the other hand, Elmer had directed him to the jazz club, and the bootlegger angle had to be investigated. Rules or no rules, Roland was certain to be pegged as a G-man if he went into a speakeasy and asked for lemonade. He could call it undercover work, and it would be within a stone's throw of the truth. "Close enough for government work," the saying went.

By the time all these thoughts had run through his mind, Roland had crossed the river, the docks, and the university campus. Uptown was newer, cleaner, and better lit than most of Arkham, and the club was bright and bustling. Roland loosened his tie, tilted his hat, and turned up his coat collar, and when he was sure he looked respectably disreputable, he approached the door. A large gentleman in a tuxedo looked him up and down, and waved him inside.

This early in the evening the place was not packed, but there was enough of a crowd for Roland to avoid standing out. He checked his hat and coat at the door and took the measure of the place. The club was decorated according to someone's idea of a Hollywood party, with a healthy dose of luxury liner thrown in. The walls were lined with long curtains of silver tinsel. Needless classical pillars were painted pale gold and rocked a little when the music grew too spirited. Fake palm trees of white ostrich feather erupted from tables painted white and silver. At one end of the room, a half-dozen musicians played Dixieland.

To the side of the stage, another large gentleman in a tuxedo stood beside a door marked "Dressing Room." A few minutes' observation told Roland that the password to the speakeasy was green and folded. Arkham was a good deal less sophisticated than New York or Chicago, it seemed. A few minutes after that, Roland was comfortably ensconced in a quiet corner with a glass of whiskey in front of him and a clear view across the smaller room.

The first sip felt so good going down that for the second time in under an hour, Roland almost forgot to feel guilty. He savored the slow warmth, held his glass up to the light, and admired the rich, amber color. This was the good stuff, all right. Leo De Luca must have connections up the coast to Canada. Roland looked around for any sign of Elmer's moonshine—"white lightning," they had called it in Jubal County—but the clientele here looked well-heeled: social drinkers rather than hardened rummies. The rotgut must move in another direction.

Another sip, and Roland felt his shoulders start to relax. He beckoned to a cigarette girl and paid over the odds for a pack of Chesterfields, scanning the crowd with a narrowed eye as he lit one.

Most of them were just here for a good time. In accordance with speakeasy etiquette, they stuck to their own groups, laughing and drinking together but making sure not to notice anyone else. The only ones who looked up were those who were here to work.

Aside from the bartender, the cigarette girl, and a couple of strategically placed bouncers, Roland noticed three other people looking around. A greasy-looking cove in dove-grey pinstripes sat at the bar, talking to an older gent. Something changed hands—all Roland saw was a glimpse of brown paper—and the fellow pocketed a thin wad of bills as his customer drank up and left. Roland dropped his eyes to his drink as Pinstripes cast a look around.

The other two were a team. They sat together as though they were on a date, but all their attention was directed outward rather than toward each other. They reminded Roland of a picture from *National Geographic* magazine: two cheetahs on an African anthill, watching for slow-looking antelopes.

The woman was in her mid-twenties, with dark, natural curls forced into a Marcel Wave and pale, natural curves forced into a tasseled red dress. Her shoes looked sharp but Roland noticed they were low in the heel: she could move fast if she needed to. He glanced at her beaded handbag, trying to estimate whether it was big enough to hold a gun. A .22, he decided, or a .32 snub in a pinch.

Her companion wore a dark suit, a thick coat of Brilliantine, and a patient expression. They were clearly waiting for someone, and that someone was not expected at any particular time. Roland wondered whether the someone was expecting them. He thought not.

Roland finished his whiskey and ordered another. It was a fine line: drink too fast and he would be slowed down, perhaps fatally, when the time came to act; drink too slowly and the staff would get suspicious, which was never a good thing in a place like this. Just as his drink arrived, the door opened and a young flapper came in. She was solo, which was not typical of her ilk, and her face looked strangely familiar. It took Roland a minute or so to recognize Edie Talbot, the tweedy magazine writer he had spoken with earlier in the day. He started to blame the whiskey for dulling his wits, but on second thought he doubted her own mother would recognize her in that getup.

She looked as though she were stepping into the Cotton Club rather than a small-town speakeasy. A turquoise plume danced above a silk helmet of the same color, perfectly matching a knee-skimming, beaded dress set off with a double rope of beads. A few heads turned, but she ignored them and scanned the room coolly. Not finding whomever she was looking for, she ankled over to the bar and settled herself on a stool. A tall, heavily iced measure of gin appeared at her elbow as she fitted a cigarette into a holder that was only a little shorter than her arm.

Pinstripes materialized at her side with a gold-plated lighter and a smile like Rudolph Valentino swallowed an accordion. She favored him with a chilly smile, but he was clearly used to rejection and settled in to wear her down.

Roland sipped at his whiskey to cover a smile. He was tempted to intervene, but she knew he was a Fed and in this company that could be bad for his health as well as his investigation. Miss Talbot was used to New York, so she could probably handle a small-town masher like this guy. He thought of the earnest, tweedy woman from the hotel lobby with amusement. She was clearly a woman of many parts, and he should not let himself forget that if their paths crossed again.

To Roland's surprise, Pinstripes seemed to be getting somewhere. Now and again, Miss Talbot would grant him a word or a nod in response to something he said. She was not exactly leading him on, but she was not giving him the brush-off either, and he was clearly prepared for a long siege. After a few minutes she turned a little toward him; a minute later she favored him with a raised eyebrow. She asked a question, and he grinned even wider and thumbed his own chest. Whatever she was looking for, Pinstripes was her man.

Pinstripes signaled the barkeep for another round of drinks, and when they came back he talked in the man's ear. The barkeep looked surprised, and then Pinstripes talked some more and got a reluctant nod in return. A few greenbacks changed hands and the barkeep went out back, returning a moment later with a nod for his benefactor.

Just as Roland was wondering what seedy delight Pinstripes was in the process of organizing, another man came out of the back. Roland's first thought was that this fellow could almost make it in moving pictures: he was tall and well built, with chestnut-brown hair swept back from a strong face. He was in shirtsleeves, dressed for work rather than for going out, and he made quite a contrast with the lounge lizard who had summoned him.

Miss Talbot clearly thought so, too. Roland could not see her face as she turned to the new arrival, but he felt a momentary pang of jealousy at the way her back straightened when she saw him. Then a few things happened at once.

The handsome fellow's smile slid from his face as he looked beyond Miss Talbot to Marcel Wave and her broad-shouldered friend. He nudged the bartender, who reached beneath the bar and came up with a sawed-off shotgun. Taking his cue, the tuxedoed gorillas at the door started toward the unwelcome pair.

The two interlopers looked around them like cornered animals. Pinstripes had just figured out that something bad was about to happen and was edging out of the line of fire as fast as he could shuffle, leaving Miss Talbot alone at the bar. So much for chivalry. Roland instinctively reached for the .38 revolver under his jacket, but kept it out of sight. There was no sense in making a tense situation worse.

Marcel Wave dipped her hand in her handbag and came out with a nickel-plated .32 just in time for one of the bouncers to grab her wrist and point it at the ceiling. The palooka's other arm wrapped around her waist and lifted her off her feet. Her knight in worsted armor looked at the shotgun in front of him and the second bouncer approaching from the side, and he weighed his chances for a long second. In that second, Roland made his move.

Two loping strides took him to the bar. He half-tackled the writer and his momentum carried them both out of the line of fire. His movement, and Miss Talbot's shriek of surprise, broke the tableau: there was a scuffle and a curse, the smack of knuckles on flesh, and a clatter of footsteps toward the door. When Roland looked up, the unwelcome pair was gone and the two doormen were heading after them, one with a pronounced limp. The barkeep's eyes were on Roland but his hands were uncertain of where to point his shotgun; Handsome was nowhere to be seen; and Pinstripes was cowering in a corner. Roland lifted Edie to her feet.

"Are you hurt?" He tried to ignore the way her perfume filled his head.

"I'll live, but I'm not so sure about my stockings."

Roland turned to Pinstripes.

"Put her in a cab for the Excelsior Hotel—and don't go with her." Pinstripes managed to look scared, disappointed, and offended all at once, but nodded. Roland turned to the bartender.

"Neutral party," he said, looking the man square in the eyes, "just looking out for the lady. Got a message for Leo from his buddy Elmer."

The barkeep's eyes twitched involuntarily toward the back door, confirming Roland's suspicion: Handsome was Leo De Luca the local hero, which meant that the unwelcome pair must be scouts for Johnny V. Roland made a big show of holstering his .38, and the barrels of the shotgun lowered slowly.

"I'm going to leave now," he said, locking eyes with the man. "If you want to shoot me in the back, I can't stop you." He turned and walked out the door slowly and calmly, despite every nerve in his body screaming at him to run.

As soon as the door swung to behind him, Roland circled around the building at a sprint. Leo had a lead on him, and so did Johnny V's people. Nerves were taut, trigger fingers were twitchy, and the darkened streets were a far better place for a kill than a crowded speakeasy.

Reaching the back door, Roland stopped to listen. The night was quiet, almost unnaturally so: Arkham was one of those old, old towns where the darkness seems to absorb sound as well as light. Roland hesitated, unsure of which way to go.

The crack of a gunshot made the decision for him. He pulled his .38 and followed the sound, hoping he would get there before the party was over. A couple of blocks later he heard another shot, closer this time. He skidded around a corner and ran slap into a standoff.

Marcel Wave and her friend had Leo backed up against a stack of crates in an alley. His shotgun was sawed off shorter than the bartender's, giving it a lot of scatter. The out-of-towners tried to spread out, but in that tight space a two-barrel blast had an excellent chance of hitting them both. The dame had her .32 and her friend was hefting a big, black Colt .45.

Roland fired before anyone could react, getting rid of the big Colt and sending its owner skedaddling down the alley clutching his wrist. Roland pointed his gun at the moll with the .32.

"Drop it," he said. She considered the matter for a little longer than he liked, but eventually let the pistol fall. Roland looked over at Leo, but left his gun pointed at the woman.

"I saw your pal Elmer this afternoon," he said. "He gave me a message for you. If you blow a big hole in me, you'll never get it." Leo searched Roland's eyes, and then gave a tight nod. Clearly, he had no idea that Elmer was no longer capable of giving anyone a coherent message.

"All right, then," Roland said. "Let's keep this short. You—," he nodded at the woman "—are pals with Johnny V down in Boston, and Leo here doesn't want to roll over and play nice. That about the size of it?"

"Take a hike, flatfoot! Yeah, that's right; I got you pegged, and I ain't sayin' nothin'!" Her eyes would have thrown fire at him if they could.

"Suit yourself." Roland gave her a shrug. "I'm not from the Prohibition Unit anyhow. I'm just trying to figure out why Johnny would blow up a whole orchestra from New York. I heard they were the types to make great customers."

"What orchestra?" she spat back. "You're all wet!" As soon as the words were out, her eyes went down and her mouth went tight. She had spoken despite herself, and that convinced Roland that she was telling the truth. He bent an eye over to Leo, who looked equally confused.

Roland pretended to consider her words while he decided how to end this standoff. The Boy Scout clamored to run them both in, but he was alone and Leo was still armed. For all he knew, the wounded gunman had gone for help and more of Johnny V's troops would arrive any minute. The book was no help to him here; he would have to choose the least of all evils.

"Get out of here," he said to the moll. "Go find your friend and go back to Boston. Tell Johnny the Bureau of Investigation's in Arkham because some rich lady's mansion went boom, and they'll be around for a while. He'd be well advised to let things cool off a little. Now scram, before I change my mind."

The woman gave Roland a look like a fisherman who had just had a thirty-pound trout jump up and kiss him. She took one hesitant step, glanced back, and then was out of the alley faster than a bullet in the back. Roland turned to Leo.

"I'd prefer not to be here if she comes back with reinforcements. Where can we talk in private?" Leo said nothing. The barrels of his shotgun came up a hair.

"Now, now," said Roland, raising his .38 squarely into the bootlegger's face. "That hurts my feelings. Didn't I just run off the opposition for you?" The shotgun stopped moving, but Leo's face did not soften.

"Just so you know," said Leo, "I flatter myself that I had things under a pretty good measure of control back there at the club. Those two were no more trouble than a fly on a cow's rump, until you decided to play Douglas Fairbanks. And there's also your federal affiliation to consider, which isn't meant to be comforting to the likes of me, now, is it? Not to mention—"

"—not to mention that you don't know what I might have done to poor, addled old Elmer," Roland finished the sentence for him. "I get it. But right now the question is, do you want to be here if she comes back mob-handed?"

"A change of scene sounds like a fine suggestion to me," Leo conceded, "although I'm not overkeen on continuing our chat in a police station, if that's your thinking. And I'll keep ahold of my shotgun, if it's all the same to you. Or even if it's not."

"Fair enough," said Roland. "We're just two new acquaintances, taking the night air and talking as we wander. Pick up the .45, too, if you like. I'll take the .32. No sudden moves, that's all." Keeping an eye and a gun on each other, they picked up the goods as slowly as two circling tomcats. Leo nodded down the alley, and they moved cautiously forward.

"I know nothing about that mansion," Leo volunteered. "Let's make that plain from the start."

"I figured as much," Roland said. "Where were you when it went up?"

"Reading the Bible to my ailing grandma. She's taken awful bad with the damp at this time of year, and the sound of Scripture brings her comfort."

"Serves me right for asking," Roland admitted. "Seems Elmer was at the mansion, though, and he saw everything. It shook him up real bad."

"And how bad would that be?" Leo's tone darkened. "If you've done anything…"

"Not me," said Roland. "The sheriff swept him up and he's in the asylum right now."

"The asylum? Lord save us." There was shock in Leo's voice, and a touch of fear, too.

"Yeah. Just staring at the wall till I mentioned you. He seems to like you."

Leo sighed softly. "He was a good man once, although not the master distiller he thought himself. It was his own hooch made him soft in the head, but he was never certifiable."

"Must have been some shock, then," said Roland. "Did you see the mansion lately?" Leo shook his head.

"A casualty of your little bootleg war, I figured," Roland continued. "It would take a truckload of dynamite to do that much damage. Anyone else around here in the import-export business and able to lay their hands on that much explosive?"

"And what possible reason would I have for giving you everything on the local trade, chapter and verse, for the asking?" Leo shot back. A sneer twisted the side of his mouth. "It's certainly not the pleasure of your company or the charm of your conversation. No, let me see if I can guess." He held up a hand and counted on his fingers. "In the first place, you saved me from those two and I now owe you my life: a weak argument, since you did nothing of the kind. Of course, you want me to understand that Johnny V's the big prize, and I'm just a charming local rogue who's doing no harm to anyone. Indeed, we're getting acquainted, and you've decided to like me and turn a blind eye to my business so long as I repay you with sweet words and useful intelligence: an offer I wouldn't trust if it came on oath from the Holy Father himself. And then, there's the prompting of your tender heart, which urges you to spring Elmer from the madhouse, just so long as I give you a measure of cooperation in proportion to your trouble." He turned back to Roland with a grin. "Was there anything I missed, or is that the sum of your argument?"

Roland considered for a moment. "Just one more thing," he said. "Assuming we don't kill each other before this conversation is over, which I would rather avoid, I can place one long-distance phone call and have a few dozen Prohibition agents tearing the city apart by lunchtime tomorrow. Starting with your speakeasy back there."

Leo thought this over for a moment and then sighed.

"And you'd threaten such a thing after drinking my whiskey," he said. "It's true that you government men have no souls. Ask your questions, then, though you'd best hope as I do that I don't live to regret my choice." The shotgun vanished beneath the bootlegger's coat, but he kept the .45 in his hand.

As they walked, Roland learned a thing or two and came to suspect a couple more. The first was that Leo had grit. Despite the fact that he was gun to gun with a federal agent, he kept a cool head and gave almost nothing away regarding his own operation. He said he did not have dynamite on hand, but admitted that he had been thinking of investing in a few sticks in case things turned heated with Johnny V's people. He also said he had heard Johnny blew up a couple of places in Boston while he was eliminating the competition there. He neither admitted nor denied supplying the orchestra with enough booze to float a battleship, and he absolutely refused to be drawn out on the reasons why the local police took no interest in the Nightingale Club, or in any other business dealings Leo might have in and around Arkham.

They were approaching the river docks when Leo stopped and turned to face Roland.

"This is where we part ways," he said firmly. The .45 made an ominous bulge in his coat pocket, pointing right at the G-man's stomach. Roland gave a grunt of amusement.

"What, you don't want me to walk you to your door?"

"You know better than that. Johnny or no, we both know which side you're on. I'm in a generous mood, though, so here's how it's going to be: I'll watch while you walk away, and you have my word that I won't shoot you in the back unless you do something I don't like the look of. That's a better deal than you'd get from most in my profession, and you'd be well advised to take it." Roland mentally filed away the fact the Leo likely had a place somewhere by the docks, turned around, and started walking.

Chapter 7

The walk back to the hotel reminded Roland just how tired he was. It had been a long, long day. The stairs to his room felt like Mount Everest. Closing the door behind him, he eased off his shoes, threw his jacket over the back of a chair, cursed when he remembered his coat and hat were still checked at the club, and fell face down on his lumpy bed.

It was still dark when his eyes opened. The music had woken him—or was it the dream? Or was the music a part of the dream, or the dream a part of the music? He shook his head to disperse the cold, damp slab of dread that was lodged between his ears, and he fumbled for the light.

Fragments of the dream still clung to him. It had been cold, colder than he ever thought possible. There was no ground beneath his feet, just the night sky all around with stars in unfamiliar patterns. The music had drawn him, pulled him to that place—that no-place—as though it were a physical force. A formless and monotonous piping enveloped everything, its random notes somehow familiar. In the dream Roland had looked around for the source of the noise and had glimpsed the strange, unnatural pipers gyrating slowly in a blasphemy of dance—and he had seen the vast and formless monstrosity around which they circled.

Roland rose from the bed and looked around the room, desperate to fix on anything real and solid in this world that would take his thoughts away from the memories of the nightmare. His jacket and shoes were still where he had dropped them; his valise stood at attention beside the small and slightly battered table with its paunchy lamp of dull brass. He strode over, turned the desk lamp on, and then went to the switch by the door. The extra light was comforting, but the haze from the nightmare still lingered in his mind.

He hesitated a moment at the window. The air outside would be cool and bracing, he knew, but the thought of sticking his head outside into the darkness roused an inexplicable dread. Shaking his head and cursing himself for a fool, Roland wrenched the sash up and thrust head and shoulders out into the night air.

A few deep breaths cooled his imagination down. Roland listened intently, giving his mind something else to focus on: he could hear the rustle of the wind through unseen trees, the distant yowl of an alley cat—and beyond it, something that undid all the good work of burning lights and fresh air.

It was that music again. Although it was very distant and only audible in brief snatches, Roland knew it immediately. The same music that had haunted his dream—and the same music, he now realized, that he had heard drifting across the lake the previous morning. Roland tried to tell himself that he was imagining things, that the formless piping was nothing more than random shreds of sound that his mind was putting together under the influence of the dream, that no sound could possibly travel from the lake all the way to the heart of Arkham: his mind knew that this must be the case, but his ears, and some deeper part of him, clung to the irrational belief that the half-heard piper from the lake was still playing—had never stopped playing, perhaps.

With no clear idea of what he was going to do, Roland pulled on his shoes and jacket and crept from the hotel. All was dark and quiet downstairs; the clock above the reception desk read a little after two. Half-dreaming still, he followed the snatches of weird piping through the dark and shadowed streets.

He paused at the city limits, listening for a hint of the mindless music to direct him further. It was with a paradoxical mix of dread and relief that he heard it again. It was coming from the direction of the distant lake.

The journey to Pine Beach had taken a few minutes by car. On foot, Roland slogged along semiconscious, much as he had slogged through the mud of the Marne, seeing nothing and thinking of nothing beyond taking one step and then another. He stumbled along the road almost blindly, barely noticing the dark trees that crowded the roadside and hung over him like the vault of some ancient cathedral, reducing the sky to mere shards of lesser darkness. All his attention was focused on the sound: he heard it more frequently now, and more clearly too, and it drew him with a strange, almost hypnotic power.

A pair of tall shadows loomed out of the darkness, strange and misshapen. As Roland's stiff legs brought him closer, he recognized the freestone pillars flanking a dirt drive. His groping hands found a carved plaque and traced out a name: Lakeview. Dimly remembering his journey in daylight, he turned away and kept walking. Hours seemed to pass; the bizarre piping continued, neither closer nor farther away. He passed by another pair of pillars, and another, until he saw "Pine Beach" written in iron scrollwork against a sky of hematite. Without pausing, he turned and walked along the rutted track.

The ruins were faintly silvered in the starlight, all their colors flattened down to shades of grey. The debris that surrounded them bobbed and jutted strangely in the gloom, and more than once Roland fancied that he saw a skeletal arm or leg reaching up to drag itself free of the chaos. The remains of the fountain gleamed obscenely white, like a broken tooth. He found himself standing by the same tree he had noticed earlier, looking at the metal fork that sprouted from its trunk.

The piping drifted across the lake in ripples, seeming nearer and then farther, then nearer again. Roland found himself on a wooden jetty without knowing quite how he had gotten there. He had been so deep in the thrall of the repulsive music that it seemed only by chance that he had not walked right off the end and into the lake. Stopping himself, he turned this way and that, trying to locate the source of the piping, but without success. It seemed to be all around, somehow coming from every direction yet also out of reach.

Retracing his steps to dry ground, Roland started walking along the shoreline. The surface of the lake seemed to amplify the sound, but he still had no sense of being any closer to its source. He walked like a man in a dream; a dim and distant part of his mind wondered whether he was still asleep in the hotel. Perhaps he had merely progressed to a different level of dreaming. Certainly, the blend of inexplicable horror and powerless fascination that the hideous music inspired in him smacked more of nightmare than reality. And yet, another part of him recognized that if he did not track this unnatural sound to its source he would surely lose his mind. Without some form of resolution it would haunt him for the rest of his life, and he would never sleep peacefully again.

So he followed the sound, stumbling through the gloom like a drunkard. He did not know how long he walked, but slowly the hideous whine of the pipes became louder. He stumbled upon a trail of sorts; bushes and undergrowth were flattened as if something large and heavy had rolled over them. Some instinct told him to follow the trail, even as a deeper part of his mind screamed at him to turn his back on it and run.

The trail twisted and turned, seemingly at random. With every step he took, though, Roland felt a growing certainty that he was closing with the source of the noise. He followed the trail around a clump of trees and up a low ridge. As he stood on the top, he saw the piper at last.

What the creature was, Roland could not say. It bulked oddly in the dim light, and he felt strangely grateful that the scene was not better lit. If he had seen the thing clearly, he might have lost his mind entirely.

Before he knew it, his gun was in his hand and he was firing as fast as he could. He emptied the magazine and pulled the trigger three more times before he realized that he had no more bullets. Then he turned and ran.

The creature ignored him completely. He saw his bullets strike its gelatinous flesh, but it kept rolling on its way and it piped its unspeakable tune without missing a note. The muzzle flash burned hideous images of the creature into Roland's mind, like the flickers from a hellish movie: the toadlike bulk; the rippling, blubbery skin; the inexplicable appendages that rolled it along; and the long, flaring pipes that might even have been part of the creature's anatomy. As he fled through the woods, those nightmare visions kept on flashing before his eyes, goading him faster and faster until there was nothing left of him but the need to run and run and never stop.

Branches lashed at Roland's face as he ran, and brush snatched at his legs. He ran on, willing himself into wilder and faster motion, hoping that his sleeping body, safe back in the hotel room, would begin to thrash sympathetically and force him to wake up.

Eventually Roland found himself at the lakeshore. He saw a boathouse in the distance. Some tiny remaining grain of reason associated this with human habitation, and human habitation with a measure of safety. Behind the boathouse stood a house, and behind that, a driveway, which led to a road. The road led him back to Arkham.

The old town's shadows seemed no less sinister, yet Roland found their human architecture comforting after the stark unreason he had seen in the woods. Somehow he was walking rather than running; his returning sanity told him that he must have stopped running some time ago, that the human body could not sustain such exertion for long, but he could not remember slackening his pace. Finding his gun dangling useless from one hand, he holstered it and staggered back to the hotel. He needed to get back to his bed, he told himself, because that was where his sleeping body was. He must get back there so he could wake up, so he could find his way back to the real world of science and reason, the world where everything made sense and horrors did not pipe in the woods.

Chapter 8

The soft tap at the door made Roland twitch a little but did not properly wake him. It was the young woman's gasp that brought him to full consciousness.

"I'm so sorry," she stammered. "I thought…" Roland blinked twice and she came into focus: mousy looking, about nineteen, and wearing a maid's uniform. A couple of brush handles sprouted from the metal bucket in her hand.

"What time is it?" The maid stopped backing out of the room, but her eyes did not get any less wide. Roland realized with relief that he was fully dressed. He must have just fallen right over when he got back from the speakeasy.

The chambermaid's brow wrinkled in thought. "It was ten when I started," she said. "I never start before, in case folk sleep late. But I…" Roland's involuntary curse sent her scuttling from the room.

He hauled himself all the way upright, wincing. Everything ached. His head felt like Jack Dempsey was inside trying to get out.

He grabbed his wash kit and lurched along the passage to the bathroom. The mirror told him he looked as bad as he felt, and he couldn't escape the feeling that it enjoyed doing so. He had broken a few rules last night and a couple of laws into the bargain; maybe this pain was the price he had to pay. It took forever to wash and shave.

Back in his room, Roland took rueful stock of his clothes. He remembered a fight—and even some shooting—but it must have been worse than he thought. His shoes were scuffed and muddy; his pants were muddy too, and torn in a couple of places. He got rid of the mud as best he could and fixed the worst of the tears with the small sewing kit he always carried. The result would not pass close inspection, but it would have to do for now. Then he dragged his aching bones and roiling stomach to the diner for a late—very late—breakfast.

The waitress was as inquisitive as ever, but Roland could not have given her anything if he had wanted to. If the truth were known, he could barely form a complete sentence. He could only trust that ham, eggs, and coffee would get his mind working again.

Back in his room, he picked up his valise and prepared to keep beating his head against the case file. If he knocked hard enough, perhaps something would shake loose and make sense of the few things he had learned since his last attempt. The feeling that he was waiting for something nagged him until he remembered that he had requested Boston's files on the two bootleggers.

He shuffled the papers he was holding, intending to put them back down and go to see whether the files were waiting for him downstairs, but then something stopped him: a faint trace of perfume, slightly familiar. He lifted the papers to his face and sniffed. It was faint, but it was definitely there. Then he sat bolt upright and cursed. It was the same perfume he had smelled on Edie Talbot when he tried to get her out of the fracas at the speakeasy. He stuck his face into his valise and sniffed again. The perfume was there too, beneath the smell of leather.

Roland flung the door open like a gunport and headed for the stairs. That sanctimonious old relic of a manager was going to get a piece of his mind. *The staff of this hotel is under strict instructions to respect our guests' privacy.* Roland would jam the hotel's policy as far down that chicken neck as it would go. Then perhaps he would ask if those reports had arrived.

He was partway to the stairs when the little chambermaid emerged from a room. She gave him a frightened look, and suddenly she became very interested in her bucket and brushes. That was unwise because it made Roland shoot an involuntary glance in the same direction and notice the bottle neck poking out from behind a feather duster.

All the anger and frustration of the past couple of days came welling up again at the sight of a more-or-less legitimate target. A part of Roland knew he would hate himself later, but for the moment that part was in the minority. He grabbed the bucket, ignoring the maid's squeak of fear.

"What's this?" he demanded. The maid backed against the wall as he thrust the bottle in her white face.

"I…I…" She struggled for words, but they had gotten clean away and left her high and dry.

"Do you make a habit of filching from the hotel's guests?" he demanded, "or are you delivering rather than picking up?" The maid looked desperately at the ground, silently pleading with it to open up beneath her feet.

Roland let the silence stretch on. He knew it would eventually become unbearable and she would have to say something. But she just kept looking at the floor. A few seconds more and her shoulders started to shake. If she started crying, she would become useless.

"All right," he said, in a softer voice. "I can see you're not Al Capone. Heck, you're not even Leo De Luca." She looked up in surprise, clearly not expecting him to know about the local bootlegger. He handed the bucket back but kept hold of the bottle, waving it back and forth to punctuate his words. She could not tear her huge, scared eyes away from it.

"I tell you what," he continued, "I'll give you back your grandma's rheumatiz medicine, and we can say no more about it. Provided—"

The maid's gasp cut him off. "Never!" Her back straightened and she fixed him with what she clearly hoped was a defiant, outraged glare. "I'm not that sort—"

"—and I'm not that sort of guest," Roland interrupted. "I just want to know one thing—no, two things. If I like what you tell me, I never saw this bottle. And you," he added, "never saw the state I was in this morning. Is it a deal?"

The maid's eyes were almost back to their usual size, but her face was still pale. She nodded silently, and the bottle found its way back into her bucket.

"First question," Roland said. "When did you let the lady from New York poke around my room?" He waved away her protest. "I know she was there. You don't use her brand of scent."

"Yesterday," the maid said sullenly. "I was cleaning in there and she gave me three dollars." Her eyes widened with a sudden thought. "Say, she didn't steal nothin', did she? She only wanted to look around, she said. I ain't no thief! Honest I ain't!"

Roland knew he had better ask his second question before the maid's composure abandoned her entirely.

"No, she didn't steal anything. Now—what's your name?"

"Hannah," the maid said miserably, "Hannah Stowe. Officer." Her eyes had fallen to the carpet again.

"Now, Hannah," Roland said, "I want you to think back four months or so." Hannah looked puzzled, but nodded. "Do you remember that composer fellow who stayed here then? What can you tell me about him? Where did he go, who did he see, and who came to see him?"

"I only saw him here," she said. "I don't know where people go."

"All right," Roland persisted, "but you cleaned his room, didn't you? Maybe you saw something and you don't know it."

"Oh, I saw plenty," Hannah said. Roland guessed from her tone that Haldane had given Arkham's gossipmongers plenty to chew on. He nodded, but she didn't need much encouragement.

"In the first place, he didn't even want his room cleaned," Hannah continued. "He had papers everywhere, and he didn't want them disturbed. Mr. Pendergast insisted, though, because he could have set the room on fire and there were the other guests to think of. But Mr. Haldane, he gave me a few bucks to leave the papers alone. I just made the bed, emptied the ashtrays, and took out the empty bottles."

"What kind of papers?"

"A lot of music paper, I guess. That was most of it. There was a big drawing he fixed to the wall with thumbtacks. It was kind of creepy, like something from a museum."

Roland remembered that Edie Talbot had said something about an inscription that had inspired the work Haldane was rehearsing. He would have to ask her when he confronted her about her snooping.

"Did it have writing on it? Hieroglyphs, anything like that?"

Hannah thought for a moment. "Maybe," she said. "But it wasn't like any writing I ever saw. Little triangles all over, like birds had walked on it." That meant nothing to Roland, but he filed it away for future attention.

"That's all you remember?" Hannah nodded once, and then her eyes widened a little.

"No!" she gasped. "There was a letter—right next to the drawing—from the university!" She beamed at him, temporarily forgetting how much trouble she thought she was in.

"The one here in town?"

Hannah nodded happily. "Miskatonic University," she said, as proudly as any alumna. "Why, I'll bet he was talking to someone there about that creepy old drawing! Those professors are awful clever with rare old languages, you know!" Roland gave her a smile in return.

"Thank you, Hannah," he said. "You've been a great help. I'll keep my word about that bottle—"

Her triumphant smile slipped a little at the reminder.

"But if Miss Talbot asks you for a peek at my room again, you tell her to come and ask me. What did she give you, three dollars?" Hannah nodded.

"All right, then. I'll see her three, and raise three." The little chambermaid looked at the six dollars like they were the treasure of the pharaohs. Actually, they represented a healthy chunk of Roland's expenses for the whole trip. "And not a word to Mr. Pendergast from either of us. Agreed?"

"Yes, sir!" she said, "I mean, officer, detective, sir!"

"Agent," he corrected her, "Roland Banks, Bureau of Investigation." She looked at him for a moment like he was one of King Arthur's knights, and then she scurried off to the next room on her rounds.

The conversation had put Roland in a much better mood. Part of it, he admitted to himself, was because the chambermaid had been so much easier to impress than the bootleggers, the asylum staff, or anyone else he had met since coming to Arkham. He was actually civil to Mr. Pendergast when he asked whether a package had arrived from Boston, and he walked away without a peep when the old buzzard told him it had not.

Miss Edie Talbot was due for a reckoning, but that would have to wait. He sat on the bed and ran his fingers through his hair. If Haldane and his friends had not been killed by the warring bootleggers—and it seemed increasingly likely that they had not—then the university was his only lead. At the very least, he needed to find a geologist to tell him what had happened to the house's foundation and the base of the fountain. If it was not dynamite that tore the house apart—and again, the lack of burning made dynamite look unlikely—then he needed to know what did.

The drawing—inscription, whatever it was—might amount to something, or it might not. The earlier work with the Salem witch stuff had raised a stink against Haldane, Edie had said, so it was just possible that someone wanted to stop this new work from ever being heard. It was thin, desperate stuff, but since he would be at the university anyway, it could not hurt to see if he could track down whichever egghead Haldane had consulted and find out what was so special about this carving. At worst, he would be able to rule it out—and who knew, he might find himself with some new suspects.

He inspected the repairs he had made to his clothes again and decided they would pass muster. He wished he had his hat and coat, but they were still at the speakeasy and it would likely be dark before he had a chance of getting them back. He grabbed his valise just in case Edie outbid him and got Hannah to let her into his room again, and set out for the university.

Chapter 9

The campus lay across the river, in the older part of Arkham. After Roland crossed the bridge, the buildings got smaller, and darker, and closer together. Some of the streets even had cobblestones.

He passed an ancient burying ground, where worn headstones leaned at crazy angles. A huge, old willow tree crouched in the middle, looking like it might stand up and trample the surrounding cottages if it took a mind to. Roland half expected a headless horseman to ride out from behind it.

At last, Roland emerged from the dark tangle of streets and alleys and onto the broad and well-kept grounds of Miskatonic University. The university had clearly been around for a considerable time. Its buildings were a mixture of old and new, with colonial brick and timber staring across broad and leafy walks at modern stone and concrete.

Roland found a building with "Administration" over the door. The inside smelled of beeswax, floor polish, and time. A young woman sat behind a tall counter of dark wood like the judge at a witch trial, absorbed in an ancient book that was almost as big as she was. She did not notice him until he cleared his throat.

"I'm sorry," she said. "Can I help you?"

"I hope so," he said, showing her his badge. "Have you worked here long?"

"All this year," she said. "What's this about?" Roland opened his valise and fished a picture of Haldane out of the police file.

"Have you seen this man before?" he asked. "I believe he might have come to the university about four months ago, possibly making inquiries about an ancient inscription."

She studied the picture briefly.

"Oh, yes," she said. "Lord Byron."

"Pardon me?"

"Sorry—that's just something I do." She smiled. "He reminded me of Byron, the poet. Mad, bad, and dangerous to know."

"That sounds about right."

"He was killed at Pine Beach, wasn't he? With all those other musicians? Is that what you're investigating?"

"That's right. Why did he come here, four months ago?"

"He had a picture of the Tell La'anat inscription," she said. "He wanted help with the cuneiform." She smiled at Roland's blank look. "It's a writing system from ancient Mesopotamia," she said.

"Like bird's feet?" Roland asked, remembering the chambermaid's words. She suppressed a chuckle.

"You could say that," she said. "Anyway, I sent him to Professor Rice. Left at the top of the stairs, and all the way to the end. You'll see his name on the door."

"Thanks," Roland said. "Do you have any idea why he came to Arkham for this? He lived in New York, and, well, no offense, but..."

"Oh, that's easy. The Tell La'anat expedition was one of ours. Professor Rice was actually on the excavation team."

"But the inscription's in New York?"

"It was. The Metropolitan Museum was one of the sponsors, so they got to display the finds before anyone else."

"You seem to know a lot about it. Are you a student here?"

"Graduate student." She nodded down at the massive book. "And I'm making some extra money filling in until they find a replacement. Everyone knows about the expedition, though: it was a real feather in the Classics Department's cap. I hear Geology is planning to go to Antarctica, just to get even."

"That reminds me," said Roland, "I'll need a geologist as well."

He ignored her questioning look; clearly this conversation was more interesting than the huge and moldy book, but he was not here to socialize.

"Geology's in the Science building," she said, indicating a vague direction out of the door. "You can't miss it. It's…"

"A big building with 'Science' written on it?" said Roland. "I saw it on the way in. Thanks!"

Roland decided to see Professor Rice first. A broad staircase led up to a narrow landing with dark corridors leading off to left and right. The last door on the left had a handwritten card reading "Dr. W. Rice, Languages" stuck into a brass holder. Roland knocked and walked in.

The paneled office was a good size, but the clutter made it seem a good deal smaller. It looked something like a library might look, if a giant hand had picked it up and shaken it like a snow globe. A bearded, bespectacled man in his late forties looked up with surprised expression.

"Professor Rice?" Roland said.

"I am," said the man, a little peevishly, "and who are you?"

"Agent Roland Banks, Bureau of Investigation." Roland showed his badge. "I'm investigating the incident at Pine Beach, and I…"

"You found out that fatuous composer was interested in the Tell La'anat inscription," Professor Rice interrupted. "Don't tell me the Bureau of Investigation believes these ridiculous stories?"

"What stories?"

The professor snorted. "The curse that destroyed the city somehow transferred itself to the orchestra, striking them down like the Curse of the Pharaohs. Utter nonsense."

Roland rubbed his jaw. "I heard the story of the curse appealed to the composer," he said, "maybe even inspired the music he was working on, but I'm not planning to arrest any ancient ghosts. Can you confirm that Oliver Haldane came to consult you about a carving from the site?"

"I can."

"And when did he do that?"

The professor made an impatient gesture. "I have no idea. Weeks ago. I'm rather busy preparing the excavation report for printing."

"But you did speak with him?"

"Why is this important?"

"It might not be, Professor," Roland admitted, "but I need to account for all his movements in Arkham, both then and more recently. It's looking like the explosion was no accident, so I need to find out whether he made any enemies locally."

Professor Rice let out a short, bitter bark of laughter.

"Professor?"

"He was the sort of man who makes enemies wherever he goes, in my opinion," he said. "One of those irritating pseudo-Romantics who poses as…as…"

"As Lord Byron?" Roland remembered what the graduate student at the reception desk had said.

"Yes!" The professor seemed pleased with the comparison. "Exactly so. You met him?"

"No," Roland said, "but I've been hearing a lot about him."

"He was certainly irritating—and persistent. In the end I transliterated the inscription just to make him go away. But murdered, along with so many other people? I can't imagine."

"He wanted you to translate the inscription for him?"

"Transliterate," the professor corrected him. "Cuneiform is an alphabet, of sorts, used by several ancient languages. I simply rewrote the inscription in our own Roman alphabet. Translation is proving more difficult—it seems to be in an unknown language. Luckily, all he wanted to know was how the text sounded."

"So he could set it to music?"

"That is what I gathered. He also wanted to know more about the alleged curse on the city."

"I don't want to take up any more of your time than I have to," said Roland, "but in case there is some link to the excavation, would you tell me what you told him?"

Professor Rice ferreted through a stack of paper and brought out a photograph.

"Here is the inscription," he said. "The original is currently on display at the Metropolitan Museum of Art." The picture showed a large slab of dark stone, carved and polished in low relief. Panels of strange characters covered the slab, carved right over the figures beneath.

The figures themselves stood in stiff poses with their arms raised, looking across the panel to something beyond the broken edge. One held a drum, and two or three others held strange-looking rattles. At the top of the panel, near the break, something that might have been a flute jutted into the picture; only a few fragmentary lines indicated the thing that played it, but Roland found the partial image horribly suggestive.

"Why was he so interested in this particular inscription?"

"You didn't see the exhibition?" The professor seemed genuinely surprised.

Roland shook his head. "I've been—away from civilization for a while," he said.

"Tell La'anat is a remarkable site. It would not be going too far to call it unique." The irritated tone had left his voice, replaced by the erudite drone of a college lecturer. Clearly he had delivered this talk before.

"Even its name is unusual," the professor went on. "A tell, of course, is an artificial mound created by centuries of continuous occupation, with each successive rebuilding taking place on top of the ruined foundations of its predecessor, and so adding to the tell's height. *La'anat* is a modern Persian word that translates as 'cursed' or 'forbidden.' The site is called Tell La'anat today, but its actual name was lost thousands of years ago. 'Tell La'anat' is purely a description: 'the forbidden city' is as good a translation as any. Similar terms appear in various languages, in documents from the Ottoman Empire, the Crusades, the Roman Empire, the travels of Herodotus—all appearing to refer to the same city, but with no name beyond 'the forbidden city' or 'the cursed city.' The locals tell all kinds of ghost stories about the place; in fact, it was very hard to find laborers for the excavation. We had to bring them in from some distance away, and even then, they ran off constantly."

"And Haldane was inspired by the idea of a cursed, forbidden city," Roland offered. "But why did he pick this inscription, in particular?" He tried not to glance down at the part of the photograph where vague lines suggested something unholy.

"There were no other panels of any size that survived the city's destruction," Professor Rice answered. "It came from a large structure that we interpreted as a temple. In fact, it was the centerpiece of the eastern wall. Where the other stones were shattered, this one was apparently knocked flat when the wall fell, and that is what saved it."

"That's all?" Roland asked. "Just because it was the only thing left from a cursed city? What if the inscription turned out to be a no-spitting sign or something?"

The blunt analogy made the professor smile briefly. "I put that to him, more or less," he said. "I thought at first that it might be some law code, based on its length: most cuneiform public inscriptions are either law codes or accounts of battles. But Mr. Haldane was quite certain that the presence of musicians meant it was a song of some kind, most likely a hymn to some ancient god."

"That sounds like him," Roland said. "He already set a witch's spell book to music, so I suppose he couldn't resist a hymn from a forbidden city."

"If it was a hymn," Professor Rice put in dryly, "and not, as you say, a law against spitting."

"What made you think the building was a temple?"

The professor smiled a little sheepishly. "To be honest, it was because we could find no other explanation for the size and shape of the structure. It was located more or less in the center of the site, and there were no remains of any trade or craft within its walls." He lowered his voice conspiratorially. "Between us," he said, "archaeologists often use the designation 'ritual' as a synonym for 'we have no idea.' It is one of the secrets of our profession."

Roland could not suppress a smile, and his eyes dropped to the stack of photographs from which Professor Rice had pulled the image of the inscription. He snatched the picture from the top and stared at it closely.

"Don't tell me you have a better idea," said the professor. "A police station, perhaps?" His sardonic expression fell away when Roland met his eyes.

"The stone here," Roland pointed, "how would you describe it?" Professor Rice took the photograph, and one eyebrow twitched up as he looked.

"That was another unusual aspect of this structure," he said. "The city as a whole had been destroyed by burning—well, first it had been burned down, and then the ruins had been demolished in a very deliberate and painstaking fashion. But here, there was no sign of burning. No ash or charcoal among the rubble, no calcination of the stone—just a strangely smooth finish on the floor of the temple."

"What caused it?" As far as Roland could tell from the photograph, the foundation of the ancient temple looked very like the shorn-off stone of the ruined mansion.

"Several theories are being pursued," he said. "Perhaps some kind of vitrification from extreme heat…"

"You said there was no ash or charcoal."

"True, and that is a problem, but the Geology Department still thinks it the most likely theory. They say no human force could have produced this effect."

"Are they right?"

"The Archaeology Department favors the theory that the wall was cut or polished using some unknown technique…"

"Like a modern quarry saw?" The professor looked surprised.

"Yes, perhaps—although this was an early Bronze Age site with little metal of any kind, let alone the kind of high-grade steel required to make a quarry saw. Why is this so important to you?"

"The foundation of the house at Pine Beach looks a lot like this."

Professor Rice made a small, choking sound. Roland looked up to see that all the color had drained from his face.

"How was the city destroyed, and when?" Roland could not keep the urgency out of his voice. "I need to know everything you can tell me."

"It was destroyed…" he began, "well—no one knows exactly when. The cuneiform is of an early pattern, at least as old as the oldest Sumerian cuneiform from Ur. The earliest Akkadian and Elamite sources speak of the accursed city as a ruin haunted by evil spirits. The stories all say that the people of the city were wicked, and that a god stretched forth his hand and destroyed them. The city was burned by its neighbors afterward, to cleanse it of its taint."

"Which god?"

"The later sources name whichever deity the neighbors themselves happened to follow: Ashur, Ishtar, Marduk, Allah. But the earliest sources say the people of the city were destroyed by their own god, who was evil and delighted in suffering."

"And what was the name of that evil god?"

"They don't give a name. Some sources imply that the name itself is too dangerous to speak or write."

"You said the Geology Department was studying the effect on the stones?"

"I'll take you." The professor rose from his desk with the movements of a man twice his age. The two did not speak further as they crossed the campus; Roland did not hear the running footsteps behind him until a hand clapped down on his shoulder.

Chapter 10

Roland turned and found himself looking at Leo De Luca. The bootlegger seemed worried.

"I need your help, Mr. G-man," he said. "Our mutual friend Miss Talbot's run into a spot of trouble."

Professor Rice looked uncertainly from one to the other. Roland quickly shook his hand.

"Thanks for your help, Professor," he said, "but this sounds urgent. I guess I'll have to talk to your geologists another day." He trotted after Leo, who was already three paces away.

"What happened?" Roland asked, "and how do you know Miss Talbot anyway?"

"A shared interest in contemporary music," said Leo, "and in other things that lift the spirits."

"And in spirits themselves," said Roland. "What happened?"

"That hellcat from the speakeasy happened," he said, "along with her tame gorilla. They must have seen her talking with me and reasoned that she could be used to exert pressure on behalf of their boss, Johnny V."

"Talking? When?"

"Around the orchestra, sometimes. She was covering them for

a fancy New York magazine, as you probably know, and I've always had a soft spot for a pretty face and a lively wit. This morning, though, she came to me with questions about the house, and the progress of your investigation, and who knows what besides, and before I could turn her away those two jumped up like the devil from a tinker's hearth and the big fellow stuck a shotgun in my face as the hellcat wrestled her away. She said they'd be in touch and not to come after them."

"So, naturally, you thought of me—we're such close friends."

"You looked out for the lady last night, and you showed you can shoot straight. Was I wrong?"

"No," said Roland, "you weren't wrong. I don't suppose you know where they took her?"

"As it happens, I do have some idea," said Leo. When Roland raised an eyebrow, he continued, "I'm a well-liked fellow, you see, blessed with friends all over town. Usually they watch out for members of your own profession, but they will also notice a car that has a lady beating on the windows. If I were a betting man—which I am—I'd say they found Elmer's cabin, back there in the woods."

"Any of those friends of yours willing to come with us?"

"They'd be of little use," Leo answered. "They've keen eyes, but soft fists. Which left me no choice but to find you. This is me." He indicated a Model T stakebed parked at the edge of the campus, and they jog-trotted toward it. "I put a couple of shotguns under the canvas. You still have the guns from last night?"

It took Roland a moment to remember the nickel-plated .32 he had taken from the moll.

"I have them," he said, "but let's not get trigger-happy. I'd prefer to get Miss Talbot back in one single, unventilated piece."

Leo gunned the engine and peeled away from the curb.

The first part of the drive followed the same route Roland and Sheriff Engle had taken to Pine Beach the day before. Mostly to distract himself, he pulled out his .38 and checked the chambers. All six were empty.

His oath brought a sharp look from Leo, but the bootlegger kept driving. Roland had fired one shot the previous night, wounding the big gunman who followed Leo along with the tough-talking moll. That should have left him with five bullets. He had not fired a shot after leaving Leo the night before—except in his nightmare, where he had emptied his gun into the horrific piping creature. But surely, that had only been a dream: creatures like that could not exist in real life.

If Roland's gun was empty, he must have really fired on the weird piper. The thing was real—as real as the mud on his shoes and the tears in his clothes. Something unspeakable roamed the woods above Pine Beach, something that mocked reason by existing when it should not.

The truck jerked to a halt, breaking Roland's reverie. The road had come to a dead end by the edge of the lake. The ruins of Pine Beach stood a few hundred yards behind them, and a steep ridge rose up from the end of the track.

"Come on," said Leo, jumping down from the cab. "The rest of the way's on foot." He threw back the tarpaulin that covered the truck bed and picked up a shotgun, jamming a box of shells into his pocket. Then he pulled the gunman's .45 from his other pocket, checked the magazine, and tucked it into his belt.

"So close to all these houses, and no one knew the cabin was there?" Roland asked. Leo shot him a pitying look.

"And just as I was starting to have hopes of you," he said. "Are you sure you're a G-man at all?" Roland grimaced. Of course everyone who lived around the lake knew the cabin was there. It might even have been built specifically to service them. That would certainly explain why old Elmer had been on the scene so soon—had even witnessed the destruction, and lost what was left of his mind.

Leo fished a metal toolbox from the back of the truck. He opened it and pushed it toward Roland. "Help yourself to shells," he said. "There's a box of .38 Special in there too, if you're out." Nodding his thanks, Roland reloaded his .38, scooped a handful of shells into his jacket pocket, then picked up the second shotgun and followed Leo up the hill.

When they reached the top of the ridge, Leo stopped walking and checked his weapons for a second time.

"No talking from now on," he said in a low voice, "and walk quietly. We don't want them to hear us coming." He straightened up and looked around with a perplexed expression. "It's odd, this," he said. "I never heard the woods this quiet before."

It had been just as quiet the previous morning. The silence felt almost solid. No wind was blowing; no squirrels rustled in the leaves or shook the branches with their jumping; no birds sang in the trees; and no waterfowl honked, quacked, or wailed across the lake. It was as though nature had fled—or was holding its breath and praying not to be discovered.

Even though he had not consciously realized it the previous day, Roland knew now that this unnatural silence was part of the reason he had felt so uneasy—even before he had heard that piping. Treading as lightly as he could, he followed Leo along the ridge.

Elmer White's cabin was a one-room shack that leaned like a fairground funhouse. It looked as though it had been built by a gang of enterprising kids in a comic strip. Its windows were boarded up, and although the door hung crookedly in its off-kilter frame, it was too dark to see inside. Leo raised a hand and crouched behind a tree to watch the place. Roland crouched beside him.

The silence pressed in on Roland as they watched the shack. At the edge of his hearing, far in the distance, Roland fancied he could hear the weird piping again. It came and went maddeningly, as if toying with him. When he listened for it all he heard was silence, but when he focused his attention elsewhere the monotonous squeal stole in at the furthest limits of his hearing.

The footfall, when it came, sounded like a rifle shot against the enveloping silence. Leo pointed: a burly figure was approaching the shack from the opposite direction, carrying a bundle of deadfall. Roland recognized the goon from the alley even before he saw the crusted brown bandage around his gun hand. He carried the wood inside, letting the door creak shut behind him.

Roland raised an eyebrow at Leo, and the bootlegger nodded. Hefting their shotguns, they moved toward the shack as quietly as they could, trusting that those inside would be too busy making a fire to hear them coming.

Leo was first through the door. There was a gasp, a curse, and a scuffle before Roland could see what was going on. He stepped out from behind the bootlegger to see the big guy with his hands in the air and the moll crouched at bay by the stone chimney, wearing an expression that would not look out of place on a wolverine. The only thing that looked more dangerous was the wooden crate by the door. It had been built to hold a dozen bottles of beer, but two dozen sticks of dynamite, lashed together in pairs, stuck out instead of bottle necks.

Edie Talbot was tied to a chair in one corner of the shack, with a rag gag in her mouth and a fresh cut across one cheek. Apart from her and the dynamite, everything looked as though Elmer had just stepped out: the rickety, unmade bed, a warped and greying table littered with an assortment of empty bottles, and a dingy overcoat hanging from a ten-point rack of antlers on the wall. A curled and spotted calendar hung beside the coat, showing the month of September, 1912, beneath the faded image of a bare-shouldered Gibson Girl and the legend "Pacific Brewing and Malting Company, Tacoma, Washington, U.S.A."

Roland motioned with his shotgun, and the moll stood up, going to stand by her large friend.

"Guns," said Roland, "nice and easy." The moll showed her empty hands and nodded toward a leather handbag beside the hearth. The big guy opened the left side of his jacket to reveal another big .45 in a shoulder holster. At a nod from Roland, he took it out with thumb and forefinger, put it on the ground, and slid it across with his foot. Roland did not bend to pick it up, but kept both eyes and both barrels on the pair as Leo flipped a clasp knife open and bent down to cut Edie free.

Edie stood up, ripping the gag from her mouth. One quick step took her to the stone hearth, where she pulled a pistol from the handbag. It was not as big as the nickel-plated model from last night, nor as good looking, but it seemed convincing enough in the writer's hands. Roland was just wondering what sort of company she kept back in New York when she took two more quick steps and dropped the moll to the floor with a blow to the temple.

"She had that coming," Edie explained, using the gun barrel to indicate the cut on her own cheek. She hoisted the handbag and turned a hundred-watt smile on her rescuers.

"Shall we go?" she said, just as though she were talking about a picnic in Central Park.

"Not so fast," said Roland. "You'll find a pair of handcuffs under my jacket, on the left side. Why don't you put 'em on your new friend here? Unless you'd prefer to keep on pistol-whipping her, of course."

"I only owed her the one," Edie replied. "More wouldn't be ladylike." With quick, sure hands she found Roland's handcuffs, wrenched the groaning moll's hands away from her bleeding head, and pinioned her arms behind her back. Leo had already trussed up the gunman with some spare rope.

With both prisoners secure, Roland stooped to pick up the discarded .45 and then pulled the dynamite box closer.

"Did you have any more of this stuff?" he asked.

"Jeez, mister, you have trouble with your hearin' or somethin'?" A trickle of blood ran down her cheek from the goose egg above the moll's eye, but she did not seem to care. "I told ya already—it wasn't us that blew the nice lady's mansion all to bits!" Roland fixed her with a skeptical look, and she subsided a little.

"That was for this dope," she muttered, jerking her chin toward Leo, "only we never found out where he keeps his stock."

"And you never will," Leo chuckled. The moll stuck out her tongue at him, a curiously childlike gesture.

"You two are adorable," said Roland. "I guess you realize you're under arrest? I'll start with kidnapping, but I'll be happy to throw in suspected ties to organized crime, bootlegging, and waving guns around. We'll figure it all out when we get back to Arkham. Your names will do for now."

The moll opened her mouth to speak, but Edie forestalled her.

"Miss Vicky Serra," she said, "of North Boston." She held up a piece of paper she had just fished out of the handbag.

"Pleased to meet you, Miss Serra," said Roland. "Now, who's—"

This time, they all heard the strange piping.

The piping drifted through the woods, as formless and monotonous as before but closer and clearer than Roland had ever heard it. He felt suddenly dizzy, as though he might fall over, and he could not stop himself from dropping the shotgun and clapping his hands over his ears.

Leo kept his hold on his own shotgun, but dropped into a crouch in the doorway and scanned the woods with desperate intensity. Roland could tell from his face that all Leo wanted in the world was to find the source of the infernal noise and keep shooting until it fell silent.

Vicky Serra spat curses at the unseen piper, fighting with all her strength to tear free of the handcuffs. Roland looked at her unnamed companion, just in time to see him break free.

The big man's face was a mask of horror. His eyes bulged out and his mouth opened wider than Roland would have thought possible. His screams were almost as awful as old Elmer's as he pulled and pulled with his massive arms until the ropes tore. Then he ran out of the shack, right over the crouching figure of Leo.

"Maury!" Roland learned the big gunman's name at last. Vicky Serra shouldered him aside, vaulted over Leo, and set off in pursuit of her cohort. Her arms were still pinioned behind her, giving her an awkward gait, but she was quickly lost to view among the trees. Leo sent a shot after her, but it had no apparent effect. The bootlegger reloaded, almost without looking. His skin was so pale, and his jaw clamped so tightly shut, that he might have been carved from ivory.

Roland looked at Edie. Her fashionable pallor had turned faintly grey. The fine thread of blood stood out shockingly scarlet against her cheek. "What…?" Her voice was barely a whisper, but her eyes were clear. She seemed to be in control of herself.

"Take this," he said, pulling the .32 from his pocket. "Can you handle two guns at once?"

Edie shook her head briefly, as if to clear it, and took the nickel-plated gun. "I'm willing to try," she said.

"Get as far away from that sound as you can," Roland said. "Go back to the hotel, and if I'm not back by morning…"

"Not a chance," she said firmly. "This has something to do with the house, doesn't it? With Oliver?"

"I think so," Roland replied. "Just don't ask me what."

"Then I'm going to find out," Edie said. "It's my job."

"I can't let you do that," said Roland. "If I'm right about the sound—I just can't."

"Forget it, Sir Galahad," Edie shook off his restraining hand. "If you're so determined to keep me safe, come with me." She tried to twist by, but Leo was blocking her way. Roland took hold of her arm.

"All right," he said, "but we're going to be smart about this." He hoisted the box of dynamite onto his shoulder.

Chapter 11

Leo fired another shot from the doorway. Roland placed a hand on his shoulder and he jumped like a startled animal. His eyes showed no sign of recognition.

"Come on," Roland yelled, his voice unnecessarily loud. "Keep us covered!" The bootlegger's eyes flicked to the dynamite and back to Roland. He nodded tautly and the three left the shack together.

Roland turned his head this way and that, but the piping seemed to come from everywhere and nowhere. It filled the woods as water envelops a drowning man, existing as much in the minds of the three listeners as it did in the world outside. Direction and distance were somehow meaningless next to the cosmic cold and loneliness woven through the terrible dirge.

It was impossible to say how long they stood transfixed by the formless music. At last, Roland set off down the slope, his two companions trailing behind him.

They might have been walking toward the music or away from it. For hours, or minutes, they wandered at random, pushing through the weird cacophony with their shoulders set as though against a high wind. Now and again they looked up, but mostly they kept their eyes on their feet. The twigs and dry leaves underfoot were natural and banal, reassuring signs of normalcy compared to what they might see if they looked up. Even so, the rustle and crunch of their progress syncopated disturbingly with the formless piping.

After a few minutes, Roland paused and looked back. Edie's face was still grey apart from the trickle of blood on her cheek and the startling white of the tooth that bit down on her lower lip. Her arms hung limp at her sides, as if the two pistols weighed a hundred pounds each. Her arms barely moved as she walked. Leo De Luca scanned the woods like a hungry animal, his head and his shotgun's barrels always moving. There was something in his eyes that could break either way, into headlong flight or berserk violence.

Beyond his companions, Roland saw the ruins of the house. Pine Beach should have been screened in by lush trees, but those closer to the ruins had been reduced to bare sticks. The lake lay like a sheet of tarnished silver, and an occasional chimney or roof-line could be seen through the trees on the far shore. There was no wind: the trees were as still as a photograph in the motionless air. Against that overall stillness, the fleeting glimpse of motion was like a lighthouse beam.

Roland set off at a run. Whether his companions followed, he neither knew nor cared; in truth, he was only half-aware of his own motion. Like that of a child confronting a schoolyard bully, his fear had turned to rage and his rage to something like courage. Without consciously deciding to, he sang and shouted so he would not have to think about the creature from his dream, the creature he was about to confront again. Blistering invective, snatches of opera, vaudeville, bawdy barrack-room fare from his army days: anything to compete with the maddening piping.

They came upon the creature in a small hollow. Leo's face contorted into a terrible mask and he began firing and reloading, firing and reloading, over and over with an unstoppable, mechanical intensity. Edie gave vent to a banshee wail and raised both her guns, firing with eyes closed rather than look at the abomination. Roland dropped the dynamite and reached for his .38, but something stopped him from drawing and firing.

The formless, toadlike, tentacled abomination seemed unaffected by the hail of fire. Here and there its warty, gelatinous hide ripped with the impact of a shot, but just as it had done the previous night, the horror took no more notice of the gunfire than it would of a gentle rain.

Roland forced his eyes up the gully, trying to fix the creature's position without looking directly at its impossible form. Cursing like a drill sergeant, he pulled out a double stick of dynamite and lit the fuse. His throw was good; the stick fell directly beside its target. Roland hit the dirt and waited for the explosion, vaguely aware in the intervening seconds of the steady boom from Leo's shotgun and the clicks from Edie's emptied pistols.

The explosion echoed off the sides of the dell, kicking up a brief shower of dirt and debris. Roland looked up, shaking his head to clear the ringing in his ears. Leo was climbing to his feet; Edie was on the ground in a fetal position, with her arms wrapped around her head. Her stockings were shredded and thick ribbons of blood trickled down her muddy legs from countless small scratches. One of her shoes was missing, and Vicky's handbag lay where the journalist had dropped it at her first sight of the creature.

Leo laid a heavy hand on Roland's shoulder and stared desperately into his eyes. Leo's mouth moved, but Roland could hear nothing. He shook his head and pointed to his ears.

"Is it dead?" The bootlegger's voice seemed very far away, but it was clear he was yelling. He had both hands on Roland's shoulders now, and he punctuated each word with a shake.

There was a small crater where the dynamite had landed. The creature was nowhere to be seen. Roland scrambled down into the hollow, searching for any sign that they had killed or even wounded the thing. He found nothing.

Turning to look up at Leo, he saw Edie standing beside the bootlegger, staring down at him. Her hands hung limp by her sides, the empty guns forgotten in her hands. Her eyes were wide and did not quite seem to focus on him. Roland climbed back up to join them.

"It's gone," he said. It was all he could say. "It's just gone."

"But is it…?" Leo sounded desperate. He needed to be sure the thing was dead, that it would not be coming back, that he would never have to see or hear it again. He needed proof.

Roland could do nothing but shrug. If this was victory, it was hollow without the body of their foe. The woods looked normal, as though nothing unnatural had taken place, but all three of them knew those woods might never be the same again—could never be the same, until the monster had been found and its taint cleansed with fire. The oldest of rituals: burning evil to destroy it completely. Nothing less would serve to exorcise what they had witnessed.

"No!" Edie gasped and dropped to her knees, her face a mask of horror. Roland and Leo looked down at her, confused for a moment, until they heard it, too. The obscene piping was fainter, distorted perhaps by the shape of the dell, but it was unmistakable.

For a long moment the three looked at each other. The same questions filled all three minds, and they searched each other's faces for the answers.

Unlike the piping, the screams had a direction. The first was a man's scream, and it was followed by a woman's. Leo snatched his shotgun off the ground and set off at a dead run; Roland hoisted the box of dynamite onto his shoulder and followed.

"Get out of here!" he yelled over his shoulder at Edie. "Find a road, get back to Arkham!" She shook her head defiantly and matched his pace despite her missing shoe, the empty guns still in her pumping fists.

They found Vicky Serra in a glade near the lakeshore, screaming curses that would make a sailor blush. She had somehow managed to step through Roland's handcuffs so her hands were no longer behind her back, and she was throwing rocks two-handed as quickly as she could pick them up. Her target, a few yards away, appeared not to feel the rocks any more than it had felt their bullets and buckshot earlier.

The creature had seemed smaller when they looked down upon it in the dell. Now that they were on the same level, Roland could see that its body—if the shifting, greenish-purple mass could be said to be a body—was a little larger than a car, and its lashing tentacles made it seem larger still. Everything else about the creature was changing constantly: its shape, its color, the texture of its skin, all seemed to shift and bubble, as though they were looking at movie frame that had come too close to the projector bulb and was endlessly repeating the last, bubbling second of its existence.

What did not change, though, was Maury. The big man was caught in the creature's tentacles, struggling with all his might and screaming like a steer that had just smelled the slaughterhouse. His massive arms ripped one tentacle away just in time for another to wrap itself around his waist, arm, or leg, the process repeating endlessly like an obscene dance to the sound of the monstrous piping. His clothes were in shreds from the struggle, and sucker marks the size of dollar pancakes adorned his arms and torso.

Leo had skidded to a halt and was looking at the unspeakable tableau slack-jawed. His shotgun hung at his side, all but forgotten. Edie stopped beside him, similarly mesmerized.

Roland, slowed down by the box of dynamite he still carried, was the last to arrive. Dropping the box, he drew his gun and took careful aim. Perhaps there was a trick to hurting this thing: a soft spot, or at least a spot that was vulnerable at some point in the creature's shifting and roiling. If not, he would save his last bullet for Maury. He sighted along the barrel, looking for details that might betray a weakness. It was good to narrow his focus, rather than looking at the whole of the monster's impossible shape.

Seeing something that looked like an eye, Roland fired. The slug struck the creature's skin and vanished with the slightest of ripples. His second shot hit the base of a tentacle, with the same lack of effect.

A boom made Roland turn his head. Leo was reloading his shotgun. Either he had had the same idea as Roland, or he could not bear to stand by and would rather do something useless than do nothing at all. Roland was about to resume his own desperate strategy when a piercing whistle split the air.

Limping on one heel and one bare foot, Edie advanced on the creature, whistling with two fingers in her mouth like a bedraggled, jazz version of Huck Finn. She shot Roland a warning look when he reached out an arm to stop her and kept walking, slowly and steadily. Her whistle slid up and down the scale in a jarring succession of flats and minors. Now and again she was able to replicate one of the creature's formless phrases more or less perfectly. Ignoring the steady boom of Leo's shotgun, Roland lowered his own weapon and watched.

Edie's whistling was a human sound, and she could not match the foul piping precisely. Occasionally the creature's piping and Edie's whistling collided in a scraping harmonic that made Roland wince:

it was these notes, rather than the matched phrases, that seemed to have an effect on the beast. The first time, it stopped as if in thought, its only movement coming from Maury's struggles against its grip. The second time, its piping changed key subtly. The third time, it lashed out with a tentacle, farther than it should have been able to reach. Edie was thrown back like a rag doll, hitting a tree twenty feet away with sickening force. Rage made Roland fire three more shots, even though a part of him knew they were useless.

Maury's struggles were growing weaker. He was fighting for breath, his face darkening as a tentacle crushed his chest. One of his huge arms strained against the grip of a smaller appendage, and his legs kicked in the air as the creature lifted him off his feet. At a place which might have been the top, front, or side of the formless beast, a nauseating, rippling movement created something that looked like a mouth. More tentacles wrapped around the fading gunman, guiding him inexorably toward the yawning maw.

Something like an electric charge shot through Roland. Before his conscious mind truly knew what he was doing, he had dropped his gun and picked up the crate of dynamite, lighting the fuses of the two sticks nearest the center. Apparently of their own volition, his feet took two steps forward and his arms swung up, lobbing the fizzing crate in an arc that led exactly where the unfortunate Maury was headed.

"Get down!" Roland heard himself yell. He caromed into Leo, bringing him down in a clumsy tackle. Vicky, he saw, stood open-mouthed for a second, watching the dynamite sail through the air before throwing herself down with a despairing wail. There was a sound like the end of the world, and everything went black.

Unconsciousness beckoned with velvet fingers, but Roland forced his eyes open. He felt blood trickle down from one ear. Everything ached as he hauled himself to his feet and looked around.

Vicky was still on the ground, writhing in apparent agony. Her eyes and mouth were both wide, and somewhere far, far behind the cacophony of tiny silver bells that filled his head, Roland could hear her keening wail. Maury was nowhere to be seen. Leo, on hands and knees, was retching and coughing helplessly; Edie was still as death against the base of the tree where the horror had thrown her. It was only then that Roland thought of the monster.

Hanging in the air above the glade was a mist, of a color that was either something more than a color or something less. There was no word for it in the language of any artist who had ever lived; it was utterly repellent, yet Roland could not take his eyes off it. The mist hung in the still air, fading slowly like the light from a guttering candle. Eventually it was gone.

Beneath the place where the mist had been, the ground was flat. Twenty-two sticks of dynamite should have produced a sizable crater—should, perhaps, have killed them all, as close to the explosion as they had been. Whatever property of the horror's body made it impervious to bullets from the outside must also have trapped the explosion inside.

Walking like a man in a dream, Roland went to the tree where Edie lay. He found a pulse; her breathing was shallow but regular. He soaked his handkerchief in the lake's cold water and blotted her forehead and neck until she stirred. There was a large knot on the back of her head, but miraculously her skull did not appear to be broken. He lifted her in his arms and directed Leo toward Vicky Serra with a jab of his chin. The tough moll seemed completely undone—whether from the sight of the monster or the loss of her cohort, Roland could not tell. She gulped and sobbed hoarsely in Leo's arms as they made their way back to the bootlegger's truck.

Chapter 12

"So, what are you going to say?"

Roland looked up from his notes to see Edie Talbot in the doorway of the borrowed office, with a notebook in one hand and a pen in the other. Apart from the healing cut on her cheek, there was no sign that anything out of the ordinary had happened to her—or at least, not until he looked at her eyes. Somehow her bright, businesslike smile did not quite reach them.

Roland gathered up his papers and covered them with a file jacket before beckoning her inside. She closed the door and sat down.

"Are you here to snoop on my investigation again?" he asked. "I should have run you in for breaking into my hotel room."

Edie held up her hands and rolled her eyes.

"Shoot me instead," she said. "Have you seen what they make you wear in a women's prison? Is that why you borrowed Sheriff Engle's office—to thwart my journalistic skills? Say, can I quote you on that?" She gazed a little over his head and waved her pen like a conductor's baton. "'G-Man Goes Gruffly to Ground, Cuts Cute Correspondent Cold.' What do you think?"

"I think I'd get posted to Alaska if I put that much alliteration in my report," he said.

Edie laughed. "Well, my readership is more sophisticated than yours. So come on, Agent, how about a quote for the masses?"

Roland leaned back in his chair and ran his fingers through his hair. "How about I crib from you this time? What are you going to say killed the New England Virtuosi? I heard all the music papers are clamoring for your story."

"Not just the music papers," she corrected him. "I've got *Time* and *Life* magazines in a bidding war by cable." She sighed, a little wistfully. "Oliver's getting more press now than ever. If only he knew."

"I'm sure he'd be proud," said Roland, "and from what I've heard of him, he'd be even prouder of going out the way he did. It was his music, wasn't it? Something he took from that inscription brought that thing here?"

Edie's smile faded and she suppressed a shudder. "I don't know what else to think," she admitted, "although did it do that to the house, all by itself?"

"Elmer said there was something bigger," Roland said, "something that just reached through from—from wherever it was. Professor Rice reckons it might have been the evil god of the cursed city. His guess is the thing we saw fell through by accident."

It was a moment before either of them could speak again.

"Too bad I didn't have my camera," Edie said at last. "Without proof, no one's ever going to believe us. Especially with Elmer and—what was the big lug's name?"

"Maury," Roland hunted through his notebook, "Maurizio Trappeto. Johnny V imported him from the old country four years ago."

"Luckily, though," Edie said, "there is still the charming Miss Serra. Or did she chew her way through the bars and bust out?"

Roland smiled despite himself. "No," he said, "some guys from the Boston Field Office picked her up before Johnny's fancy lawyers could get here. They were on the next train back, and I wish Miss Serra and my Boston colleagues great joy of each other."

"So at least you got a bootlegging collar while you were here," Edie said. "That's got to help you."

"Maybe a little, although it hasn't impressed Mrs. van Dreesen."

Edie made a sympathetic face. "Yikes," she said, "I'd almost forgotten about her. What did you tell her?"

"She'll have to read the report like everyone else," said Roland, "if I ever figure out what to write in it."

"I don't suppose you can tell the truth." Edie was suddenly serious. Roland shook his head.

"If you'd asked me that question a week ago…"

"I know," she said. "They'd lock you up, and me along with you if I told the same story. I doubt Mrs. van Dreesen's insurance company would be swayed by a story of an evil god." Roland gave vent to a brief snort of laughter. "What?" she asked.

"You know," he said, "their first report said it was an act of God. That's why they didn't pay out, and why I was sent here in the first place."

"Not quite the god they had in mind," she said, "although I doubt even Mrs. van Dreesen's policy covers her against ancient curses. The heck with it—I may just head to the Nightingale Club and get bent. Maybe the spirits will move me and I'll dream up the perfect story. Care to escort a lady?"

"I'm still a federal agent, you know."

"And you were a federal agent when you dragged me out of there the other night, as I recall. Was that whiskey I smelled on your breath, or your own special hair lotion?"

"I was casing the joint incognito. I had to have a couple of drinks, to avoid suspicion."

"Any sacrifice in the line of duty. They should give you a medal."

"Are you here to give me a hard time, or do you want to help?"

"Help? Are you putting me on the case, Agent?"

"You came here to find out what's going to be in my report, didn't you?"

"Except you have even less than I do."

"So help me write it."

"You couldn't afford my word rate."

"Consider it a trade for not running you in."

"Why, Agent Banks! Are you soliciting a bribe in-kind?" Edie's eyes widened in mock offense.

"Enough," said Roland. "We have to figure something out. Have you heard from Leo? What's he saying?"

Edie shook her head. "He's taking a trip, is what I heard. He took off as soon as we got back, without a word to anyone. The boys at the Nightingale think he's in Canada buying stock. Or maybe the Bahamas."

"I can't say I blame him. A bracing sea voyage does sound good right now."

"I'll meet you on the lido deck," she said. "So, assuming we don't mention—you know—then what kind of story makes sense? Some kind of explosion?"

Roland shook his head. "That was the first thing I thought of, but it won't fly. There was no gas on site, and the boiler was too small to level the entire house. I thought maybe the orchestra could have been running a still of their own—"

"They did like a gargle," she put in.

"—but it would take a commercial-size still to make a big enough explosion. Besides, none of that can account for the second explosion."

"Second explosion?"

"I think you missed it. It happened right after your argument with that tree."

"Oh, right," said Edie, involuntarily putting a hand to the back of her head. "What about the dynamite? Can you pin it on Johnny V?"

Roland shook his head wearily. "I spent all morning trying to figure out a way to do that," he said, "but it's just not adding up. The dynamite's gone, so I can't produce it in court, and besides, I'd have to put Miss Vicky in the witness box. Who's to say what she might come out with?"

Edie let out a *pfft* of air. "Who cares? She's getting locked up whatever she says, I imagine. In an asylum if she tells the truth—in jail, otherwise. There has to be some room for negotiation there."

"Maybe," said Roland, "but the last time I saw her, she was cursing me out for what happened to Maury. I wouldn't put it past her to try to smear me for not taking Leo in as well as the two of them—making some case that the local boy's paying off the cops and bringing the Prohibition Unit down here poking under every rock."

"Hell hath no fury," Edie quoted, a little out of context. "I guess she really liked the big guy. But—" She turned to Roland with a worried expression. "What's to stop her from doing that anyway?"

Roland shrugged. "I'm guessing she knows better."

"What?"

"Right now, she's only facing charges for kidnapping you to put pressure on Leo. My guess is that Johnny will get her out on bail, and then she'll disappear before her trial. Some nice little island in the Caribbean, maybe, or down to Mexico, or somewhere else out of the way. But it all depends on Vicky getting bail."

"So?"

"So if she accuses a federal agent of corruption, or looks like she's willing to turn state's evidence against another bootlegger—say, Leo De Luca—then everything changes. She becomes a valuable witness for the government, and instead of bail she gets protective custody. That means that Johnny V and his lawyers can't get within a mile of her, and *that* means that Johnny won't be able to keep from worrying that she might spill the beans on him as well as on your pal Leo. All of which means that Miss Serra's life gets a lot more complicated very fast."

"I hadn't thought of that," Edie admitted. "But do you think she's smart enough to figure all that out for herself?"

"I gave her a few pointers between curses," Roland said. "She had to pause for breath now and again."

"I hope she got the message," Edie looked only half-convinced. "So what's left, an earthquake?"

"I checked with a geologist at the college, and New England isn't exactly earthquake country. The last one was in 1755—and earthquakes don't usually stop at destroying a single house."

"Sheesh, Professor," Edie looked offended. "I only asked."

"Don't blame the messenger. There might be something in the geology angle, though."

"I'm all ears."

"What if there was some kind of underground gas pocket? Suppose it leaked into the house and blew it up?"

"That sounds good!" Edie said. She chewed the end of her pencil as she thought. "How about this? It must have continued to escape and build up, because when we were chasing those bootleggers a stray spark from a ricochet or something set off the second explosion!" She started writing rapidly. "And that whistling noise—"

"Don't remind me." Roland shuddered at the memory.

"—that was caused by gas escaping through fissures at various points in the woods." A triumphant expression stole across her face. "And since the whistling's stopped, we can be sure there's no more gas escaping. Everyone's safe, and no one has to worry about their own lake houses going boom!"

Roland thought about this for a minute.

"That does cover pretty much everything," he said. "Where do you think that will leave Mrs. van Dreesen?"

"Off your back, and onto someone else's," said Edie. "My guess is the insurance company will cite natural causes and keep on refusing to pay, so her lawyers will try to find someone else to blame. Could be a local mine or quarry, if there is one, or even the Worthington estate for selling her a house on top of a gas pocket."

Roland gave a grunt of amusement. "She'll spend more on lawyers than it would cost her to rebuild the house," he said.

"Oh, probably," said Edie, "but the thing you have to understand with her type is, it's never about the money. Worrying about money is vulgar. You keep going until you've won, no matter what it costs."

"I just hope this works," Roland said. Something in his tone made Edie look up.

"Why wouldn't it?" she asked.

"I don't know," he sighed. "Making up stories, lying in an official report—it just doesn't feel right."

"What's the alternative? Tell the truth and get locked up? Even if we had undeniable proof…" She let the sentence trail off.

"I guess you're right," Roland conceded. "But don't we have a duty—shouldn't people know?"

"What good would it do them if they did? Do you feel happier for knowing? I know I don't."

"I know," he said, throwing up his hands. "I know. It's just that—well, my whole career I went by the book, never put a foot wrong. I told myself I was just trying to stay out of trouble, that federal agents had to hold themselves to a higher standard. But ever since I got here…"

"That's Arkham," said Edie.

Roland looked out of the window. "Sheriff Engle said something similar, when I first got here," he said. "There's just something about the place that's off somehow."

"I know I'll be glad to get back to New York," said Edie. "Hell's Kitchen looks positively welcoming after all of this. How about you? What's next for the fearless G-man?"

"It looks like I'll be sticking around," Roland said.

"Sticking around? Does someone really hate you that much?"

"Something's off about this place," he repeated. "Sheriff Engle knows more than he's telling, and so do those eggheads at the university. I get the feeling that what we went through is just a taste of whatever's wrong around here. If I cut and run, then my report is just a lie—nothing more. We can talk about protecting people from a truth the world isn't ready for, but really I'm just ducking out."

"What does the Bureau have to say about that?"

"That's the strange thing," Roland said. "I got a cable from the Boston Field Office saying I'd been seconded to a special agency of some kind. No name or anything—just orders to stay here, keep my eyes open, and wait for further instructions. I get the impression that someone in the federal government has a clue what's going on. Maybe I'll get some answers."

"Or maybe you'll get killed or driven buggy," Edie said. "That would be too sad, because I've kind of gotten to like you." She gave Roland a pretty little pout, and he laughed as he felt his cheeks redden.

"Come on, is anyone really that much of a choirboy?"

"Boy Scout."

"Say what?"

"That's what they used to call me," he said. "The Boy Scout. I used to believe it, too, but now, I don't know what I am. I broke just about every rule in the book on this case."

"It can't have been much of a book, then," Edie said. "Maybe it's time to write your own. If Arkham makes its own rules, you should too."

About the Author

Graeme Davis discovered the Cthulhu Mythos in 1982 after picking up an imported first edition of Chaosium's *Call of Cthulhu* RPG. He helped develop *Warhammer Fantasy Roleplay* and *Vampire: The Masquerade*, and he has written Cthulhu Mythos gaming material for several publishers. He is also the author of a *Dungeons & Dragons* novel and several published short stories. He blogs at graemedavis.wordpress.com, tweets at @GraemeJDavis, and maintains a Facebook author page at https://www.facebook.com/Graeme-Davis-276379857250/.

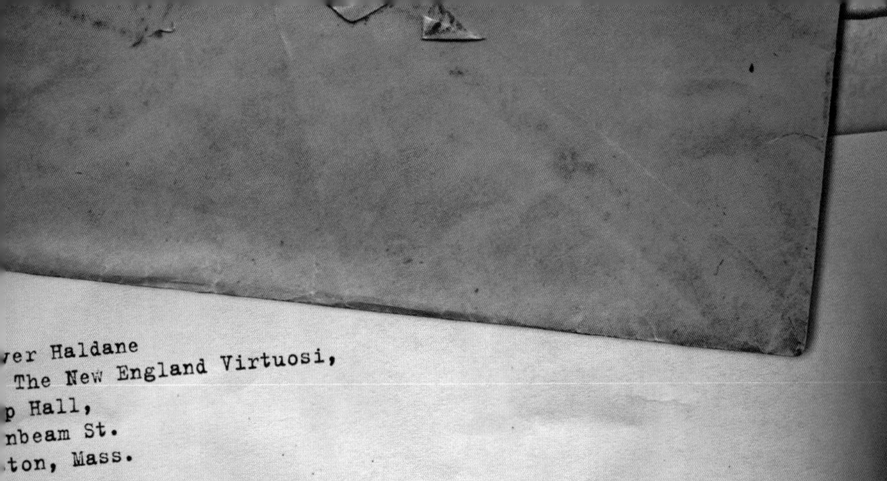

ver Haldane
The New England Virtuosi,
p Hall,
nbeam St.
ton, Mass.

ofessor Warren Rice,
partment of Classical Languages,
skatonic University,
llege St.
kham, Mass.

ear Professor Rice,

I recently had the pleasure of seeing the remarkable elief from Tell La'anat in display at the Metropolitan Museum of rt in New York City. The style of the relief, and the story of he cursed city whence it came, intrigued me greatly, and they have inspired me to begin work on a new musical piece.

The exhibit literature hinted that the panel came from a temple and showed some kind of religious ritual. Do you believe it possible that the ancient writing might constitute some kind of hymn or devotional? If so, I would dearly love to include its words—in the original language—in the libretto of a choral section.

I am told that you are the man to contact about the inscription, and it is my hope that you might spare me an hour of your time to discuss the matter. I can come to Arkham at any time that suits you.

With thanks in anticipation
of a speedy and positive reply,

Oliver Haldane

Oliver Haldane
Musical Director

DIRECTOR

Department of Justice
Bureau of Investigation
New York Field Office

MEMORANDUM

To: Agent in Charge, Boston Field Office

Arrange for an agent to be sent immediately to Arkham, MA, with orders to investigate the destruction of a lake house at Pine Beach, Chaumadgee Lake.

This matter is to be given the highest priority. One agent should suffice. A detailed report is to be sent to this office without delay.

Mrs. Edgar van Dreesen
Diedrich Building,
67th St. & 5th Ave.,
New York, NY

My Dear Hal,

I was telling Emma of my troubles at the Country Club earlier today, and she suggested I should write to you. I am sure you have read of the disaster that befell my little country place at Pine Beach last week. The loss is almost more than I can bear—it is one of my most treasure[d] gifts from my late husband, of course, and the art world may never recover from the tragic deaths of my good friend Oliver Haldane and his New England Virtuosi. They were not the Philharmonic, as you so rightly observed, but they were [...] future of music, and we are all diminished by their loss.

But enough of that. Obituaries will be written by ab[...] hands than my own. I am writing to you because the loca[l] police have driven me to despair. They seem entirely unabl[e] to account for what happened, and they have simply thrown up their hands and invoked an "Act of God"—something t[...] insurers are delighted to accept, of course, but I, rather less so.

And so, dear Hal, I appeal to you. I do trust that [I] am not imposing, and I would not have troubled you a[t] all had not your own dear Emma insisted that you would be happy to help. I do so hope you will take pity on m[e] in this hour of need.

Yours ever,
Edith

... structures above a height of approximately ... outbuildings,
... scattered over a wide area and in all directions, consisting of broken
stones and timber, furniture, and human remains (see below). Some fragments
of debris were found embedded in the trunks of nearby trees. All signs point to a
violent explosion, cause unknown.

Photographs were taken at the scene by a person staying in a neighboring house.
See Appendix A.

WITNESS STATEMENTS

There were no reliable witnesses to the explosion itself. Neighbors were
nterviewed: they reported hearing a loud noise similar to an explosion. The shock
rom the explosion was felt in Arkham, which is over 2 mi. away. Those first on the
cene reported that there were no survivors, and it is concluded that all 38 victi...
ere killed instantly.

HE HOUSE

Miskatonic County Sheriff's Office

Reporting Deputy:	Name and Offense Charged:
Earnest Engle	Explosion, Cause Unknown

THE VICTIMS

All human remains were removed from the site by the county medical examiner and held for formal identification and determination of cause of death. The human remains recovered from the site were declared to be sufficient to account for 38 individuals in total. The condition of the remains varied from almost intact to completely torn apart.

Pending formal identification, it is assumed that the remains recovered account for the 37 members of the New England Virtuosi Orchestra, as well as the New York composer and conductor Oliver Haldane. See Appendix B for full list of victims. These individuals are known to have been in residence at the house at the time of the explosion.

The orchestra members were staying at Pine Beach as guests of Mrs. van Dreesen while rehearsing a new musical work composed by Haldane. The question of whether they caused or contributed to the explosion cannot be answered conclusively at this time. During their stay at Pine Beach, they had been involved in various incidents of rowdiness and petty vandalism. According to press reports, Haldane was personally acquainted with a number of self-professed anarchists in Manhattan and elsewhere. Such associations are said to be commonplace in artistic circles, and it is not known whether this is relevant to the case.

EVIDENCE OF CRIME

Based on the evidence at the scene, it is not possible to determine whether the destruction of the house and the deaths of the victims can be regarded as resulting from a criminal act. It will not be possible to make such a determination until the cause of the explosion is definitively established, which cannot be done without the services of an advanced scientific laboratory. Likewise, it will not be possible to assign responsibility for the destruction and loss of life until the cause of the explosion is established.

CONCLUSION

At the present time, the only finding that can be recorded is "explosion, cause unknown." It may be that further investigation by forensic scientists and other experts will be able to shed more light on this incident, but this office cannot speculate on such a possibility.

Signed,

Ernest Engle

Sheriff Engle

Rites of Apsu

Oliver Haldane Speaks Exclusively about His Newest Work

By Edie Talbot

OLIVER HALDANE IS NO STRANGER to controversy. His *Missa Negra* caused a furore two years ago, both for its title (which, as readers will no doubt recognize, is a reference to the Black Mass of Satan worship) and for the libretto of the choral sections, for which Haldane turned to a witch's spell book he claims to have found in Salem itself. The man is no less notorious than his work, for scarcely a week seems to go by without his name appearing either in the society pages or the police blotter.

The composer is unapologetic on both counts. "It is the duty of an artist," he maintains, "to challenge and eventually transform society into his own image, breaking down the walls of convention that hold the imagination prisoner." It would not be going too far to say that Oliver Haldane has declared war on convention, and this has brought him into conflict with the authorities more than once. He claims that J. Edgar Hoover is keeping a file on him, although the top G-man has declined to comment.

What cannot be denied is that Haldane delights in the company of types whose names might well figure in Mr. Hoover's bedtime reading. He was photographed sharing a table with Owney Madden at Harlem's swanky Cotton Club last summer, and this Thanksgiving he broke a winter trip to the Riviera for drinks at the Left Bank's notorious Lapin Agile, where he rubbed shoulders with painters, writers, and revolutionaries from three continents in the melting pot of ideas that is modern Paris.

Back in New York City, Oliver Haldane sat down with your correspondent to give readers a glimpse into his artistic process as well as a few hints about his much-anticipated new work, *Rites of Apsu*.

In contrast with the familiar Latin of *Missa Negra*, the title of the new work derives from ancient Mesopotamian mythology, in which Apsu, or Abzu, is the equivalent of the classical realm of Tartarus, the Hel of Norse myth, and indeed, the realm with which nuns and teachers have threatened generations of free-spirited children. When asked how he came by the title, Haldane explained with contagious enthusiasm.

"I was visiting the Met," he said, using the pular abbreviation for New York's famed etropolitan Museum of Art, "for inspiration, I sometimes do. I had it in my mind to research e Borgias, or possibly the Roman emperor aligula, but I wandered into a small exhibition a side gallery that showed various new finds om Mesopotamia. It was there that I read f a city that was so wicked that its neighbors estroyed it in antiquity. They destroyed lmost everything, except for one inscription hat survived by chance. Immediately I was ntrigued. Like Sodom and Gomorrah, this city vas destroyed—utterly destroyed, according to he archaeologists who found it—and the site uffers an evil reputation to this day. Before I eft the gallery, a new work was taking shape in my mind."

Haldane was unwilling to divulge anything further about the piece itself, but aficionados of his work will recognize the themes of sin and rebellion that run through most of his oeuvre to date. He did let slip that there will be a choral section that, like the notorious spell incantations of Missa Negra, is taken from an original source: in this case, the cuneiform inscription that first caught his eye in the museum. "I want to let this dead, cursed people speak for themselves again," he said, with characteristic enthusiasm. "Their neighbors silenced them centuries ago, but not forever."

Work is progressing well, Haldane confirmed. Over the coming months he will be working with his favorite members of the New England Virtuosi Orchestra at a secret location to orchestrate and rehearse the new work. When pressed, he hinted at a premiere in New York or Boston as early as midsummer.

The New England Virtuosi Orchestra has earned itself quite the reputation for its avant-garde performances **and lifestyles.** When they are not rehearsing their music, these high bohemians can be found frequenting **the restaurants** of Greenwich Village and the theatres of Provincetown, Mass.

THE TELL LA'ANAT TABLET

TELL LA'ANAT WAS DISCOVERED IN 1921 by the Miskatonic University expedition to northern Mesopotamia. This is the first Western study of this remote desert region, which stands at the crossroads of history. Over the last fifty years, discoveries elsewhere in Mesopotamia have led to great advances in the study of the world's first cities and the beginning of civilization.

The tell's name shares a root with a Persian word meaning "accursed," and it is known by similar names in documents of the Ottoman, Crusader, Early Islamic, Roman, and Greek periods. The city's true name, by which it was known before its destruction, has not yet been discovered.

At some time around five thousand years ago, the city was attacked and destroyed. The walls were razed, and buildings were burned to the ground. The layer of ash and rubble, dated by pottery shards, is at least as extensive as that found by Heinrich Schliemann in his excavation of the Troy II remains.

So complete was the destruction that only one partially complete relief survives. Found inside a building that the excavators believe was a temple, this broken section of a wall panel, approximately four feet wide and five feet high, had apparently fallen off its wall, landing face down. It was quickl ered by rubble, which apparently from the city's destroyers and it from the systematic destructio was inflicted upon every sculptu inscribed surface in the city. Othe panels in the same chamber were tered into tiny pieces, apparently the deliberate intention of dest them completely.

The relief is of carved basal appears to have been part of a panel. It is carved in low relief wit ures in the Sumerian style, and the overlaid by extensive cuneiform This style is well known from later opotamian contexts, such as the f Behistun historical relief attribut Darius the Great. The cuneiform that overlies much of this panel a to have been written in a languag is new to scholarship, and therefore yet to be translated.

The relief appears to depict a reli service in progress. A group of shipers stands at the right side o surviving fragment, looking to the with their hands raised in an attitu prayer. The deity they are worshipi apparently in an adjacent panel tha not yet been recovered.

Archaeological examination of the revealed that the city was last occ

early Bronze Age Uruk period of
ıerian culture. The city's popula-
this time has been estimated at
two thousand. Excavation efforts
ampered by difficulty of finding
The tell has an evil reputation
as a haunt of evil jinn. As a
no one from any nearby village
e persuaded to assist with the
ion, at any price. The excava-
re told by the local populace
an once that an ancient evil still
within the ruins, and that anyone
enough to set foot there risked
ry souls.

forthcoming monograph on the
gends surrounding the site, Pro-
Varren Rice of Miskatonic Uni-
vill examine the local legends as
ted folk memory of the ancient
city's destruction and as a resource for reconstructing the true history of events. Professor Rice notes that the motif of a cursed city destroyed for its wickedness is common to many traditions. The Book of Genesis, of course, tells of the destruction of Sodom and Gomorrah, and Breton folk tales recount the drowning of the city of Ys.

It is possible, says Dr. Rice, that these ancient legends reflect long-forgotten religious wars waged against minority sects by the state religions of expanding empires: if that is the case with Tell La'anat, it may be that an independent city-state with its own religion was punished harshly for resisting assimilation into an expanding empire, most likely a rising local power such as Mari or Asshur.

SPORTING NEWS —

Pittsburgh Pirates defeat the Washington Senators!

WORLD SERIES RESULTS

ARKHA

'EN PAGES

OLD WORTHING

EXPLOSION, SAY POLICE: C

Arkham, M.A., Oct. 16. (Exclusive)—The lake house at Pine Beach, known to most Arkham residents as the old Worthington House, was destroyed last Monday in what the local police and county sheriff are calling a violent explosion. The shock of the disaster was heard and felt more than two miles away in the center of town.

After the last of the Worthington family died of the Spanish flu, the house was purchased by Mr. Edgar van Dreesen of New York City, who hosted many of New York nd Boston's leading lights for summer arties and balls.

For most of this summer, the house was loaned to renowned composer Oliver Haldane and the New England Virtuosi orchestra. It was understood that the musicians sought out the solitude of Chaumadgee Lake to have quiet and privacy for their rehearsals, but as many in Arkham can attest, they have proved to be among the more outgoing visitors the town has seen in recent years. They have been accused of various forms of misbehavior, including public drunkenness, solicitation, and the destruction of a motorboat owned by Mr. Gerald Manners of Trout Bank.

Half of the house was completel destroyed; only the chimney and the lake side wall remained even partially intac Thirty-eight bodies, whole or partial, hav been recovered from the wreckage, ac cording to the county medical examine It seems that there were no survivors.

At the time of going to press, tl official explanation remains "explosic of unknown cause," with the authoriti refusing to be drawn out any furth Deputy Dingby of the Miskatonic Cour Sheriff's Office would say only, "our inv tigation continues, but it would be pren ture to make any announcements at t time. We expect a special investigator arrive soon, and we hope they will be a to shed more light on this tragedy."

The editors of this journal, and ind all the people of Arkham, look forwar the arrival of the special investigator n tioned by the deputy, and we hope his expert work will yield more det answers.

PIRATES TRIUMPH 9–7 OVER SENATORS IN GAME SEVEN

CHAMPIONS DEFEATED

kham Advert

RCE • SERVING ARKHAM, KINGSPORT, AND THE MISKATONIC RIVER VALLEY

SACHUSETTS, FRIDAY, OCTOBER 16, 1925

N HOUSE DESTRO

E REMAINS UNKNOWN

dible blast obliterated the old Worthington House on Chaumadgee Lake

nning Photographs of the Disaster

Edie Talbot is more at home at k salons than in a lake house out- kham. Readers in the know may ze her name from her reporting in agazine such as *The Musical* accomplished photographer as well as a writer, she was able to take the first photographs of the wreckage left behind by the catastrophe. Of her experience at Pine Beach, she was only able to say, "there was ... like nothing I have ever heard, and

SON

CONT
STAI

By Our

To thos of New Y brethren c notoriety pany. In C words, "t challenge are encou to free th rity of so-

Arkha er side o visitors have bee regular p understa mate, yo persuad speak o firmed was a Roman ruled o

The more s ed, wh the fat Old Te tured would early, W

…ETTS, FRI…AY, OC…

NGTON HOUSE D…

…CE: CAUSE REMAINS UNKN…

…rboat owned
…ut Bank.
… destroyed,
…ve the level

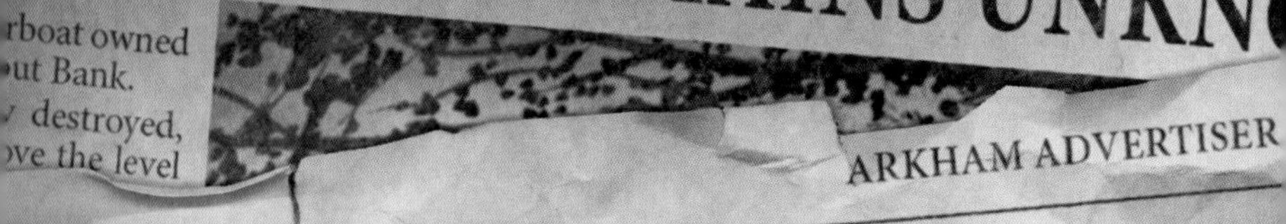

ARKHAM ADVERTISER

VAN DREESEN TO LEAVE?

…hat will become of Pine Beach now?

…n the wake of the disaster, there is …ne talk in town about the future of …e Beach. People are asking whether … house will be rebuilt, and whether its …rrent owner, Manhattan socialite Mrs. …gar van Dreesen, will sell or stay. As this …ition went to press, Mrs. van Dreesen …d not yet responded to the *Advertiser's* …lephone call requesting a statement.

Known in town as the "summer peo…le," wealthy families from Boston and …ew York own the majority of the houses …round Chaumadgee Lake. Most are are …nly here for a few weeks out of each year, …nd Mrs. van Dreesen is no exception. …While this paper has reported on several …of the parties and balls that she hosted at Pine Beach since her late husband bought the house from the Worthington estate in 1919, Mrs. van Dreesen has not been seen much in Arkham itself.

The question of rebuilding has implications beyond the world of high society. A disaster like this would make the owners of neighboring properties nervous, especially because the cause of the ex… plosion remains undiscovered. Althoug… they are infrequent visitors to town, t… "summer people" form an important p… of our seasonal economy, through th… purchases of food and other necessit… from local traders and the jobs they p… vide for housekeepers and other staff.

The loss of one house would be a m… fortune, but if it develops into a full-s… desertion of the lake, with house ow… moving their summer activities to … Hamptons or Cape Cod, some towns… may find their livings at risk. Such… least, is the fear that is running thr… Arkham's mercantile community at… time. Leading citizen Charles "C… lie" Kane warns against panic, how… "Those who know Arkham know t… has survived much," he told our rep… "and though I am sure everyone in… would wish to send their sincerest c… lences to the families of the victims … terrible tragedy, our town has su… worse, and it will survive this."

Mrs. van Dreesen is said to be i… with the house's insurers, and we c… hope that the future of Pine Beach … come clearer once those discussi… concluded.

NEW M.U. OBSERVATORY IS A …

NEW … RESOU…CES

16, 1925

PRICE FIVE CEN

ROYED, 38 DEAD

SOME BLAME THE VICTIMS

CONTROVERSY STILL STALKS ORCHESTRA

By Our Own Correspondent

To those in touch with the arts worlds of New York and Boston, these lively brethren of Orpheus have earned some notoriety for their hijinks and low company. In Composer Oliver Haldane's own words, "the duty of the true artist is to challenge laws and morals wherever they are encountered, and by overcoming them to free the human spirit from the mediocrity of so-called 'decent behavior.'"

Arkhamites with a taste for the wild side of life, along with more seasoned visitors from New York's demimonde, have been amply satisfied, it is said, by the regular parties held at the house. Perhaps understandably in the current legal climate, your correspondent was unable to persuade any of the composer's guests to speak on the record, but many have confided in confidence that Mr. Haldane is a host who could outshine certain Roman emperors, with no entertainment held out of bounds.

There are bound to be some among our more sober citizens who will be reminded, when they read of the explosion, of the fates of Sodom and Gomorrah in the Old Testament. Certainly the scene, as pictured in the accompanying photographs, would not be out of place in the life of an Old Testament pagan-smiting saint.

Whatever moral lessons might be taken from the disaster by those with a traditional frame of mind, the physical cause of the explosion remains a mystery. Authorities refuse to be drawn out on the question of whether the explosion was caused by a gas leak or by something more sinister. While our fair town remains a relative backwater in Prohibition's war on liquor, it is rumored that bootleggers from Boston are expanding their reach along the coast, and Arkham would lie squarely in the path of such an expansion. Perhaps the orchestra's low connections extended into that shadowy world, and the explosion is somehow tied to a bootleg war. No one from the Arkham City Police Department or the County Sheriff's Office was willing to comment on that possibility.

It has also been suggested that the orchestra's past caught up with them in Arkham. Among the town's coffee cake set, one can hear a rumor that would not be out of place in a Clara Bow movie. According to this tale, a wronged woman smuggled dynamite into the house's basement to carry out her revenge. As with all the best rumors, the details vary. The details of the wrong suffered by our unfortunate, hypothetical protagonist are especially changeable, becoming more or less graphic—though seldom any less lurid—according to the gentility of the teller. In some versions, the wronged woman committed suicide and vengeance was taken on her behalf by one or more relatives. In others, the victim or her family had ties to a powerful bootlegging syndicate, which neatly ties this rumor into another popular tale. One rather less satisfying account omits the wronged woman altogether, and lays the blame at the feet of a zealous but misguided evangelical of unknown origins, who walks the earth on a self-appointed crusade against the ungodly.

ANGE SIGHTINGS AT

that the structure's position within the city's walls (so far as those walls could be traced)—and the singularly thorough destruction visited upon it in antiquity—might lead to the supposition that it was originally a temple, despite its significant differences in size, shape, and orientation from known temple structures in other contemporaneous cities in the region.

The thoroughness of the destruction, it might be argued, strengthens this interpretation. As history has shown from the time of Akhenaten to the Albigensian Crusade and the Russian pogroms, there is almost no force in human history that can engender such deep and visceral hatred as religious difference, and it is clear that nothing less than the most virulent hatred could have inspired the extent and thoroughness of destruction exhibited at Tell La'anat.

As the focus of the most violent and painstaking destruction, this building must have been the object of the attackers' deepest hatred, and therefore it is not unreasonable to suppose that this was indeed the temple of a religion so repugnant to the city's attackers that it had to be reduced not to rubble but to gravel, its inhabitants not only slaughtered but burned, and the site placed under an anathema so powerful that, in various forms, it persists to this day in the tales of the cursed and forbidden city that the expedition heard so frequently in the neighboring villages.

The tablet measures 3 feet 11 inches by 5 feet 1 1/2 inches. It was found face down inside the temple perimeter and was covered by a thick layer of ash and rubble. Apart from its broken edges, the tablet is remarkably intact, and it is by far the largest single find from the city. Its position in situ suggests that it fell from the wall and was buried, which allowed it to escape the complete destruction suffered by such additional panels that are thought to have existed.

The figures are broadly consistent with the art style of the period. Some variations are sufficiently consistent with finds from nearby cities to be considered regional variations, but a few variations seem unique. Among these are certain decorative symbols on the clothing of the human figures as well as the slender object, interpreted as a ritual horn or pipe, which intrudes into the image from the broken edge at the left. Although they are too small and fragmentary to permit any confident interpretation, the curvilinear elements close by the partial instrument (described as "cloud-like" in the excavators' field notes) may constitute an additional unique artistic element.

The cuneiform text is presented in six distinct panels, each omposed of an estimated 250 characters. Some of the panels are laid over the sculpted figures, which is not unknown in the case of uneiform reliefs. The style and method of carving is consistent ith the time and region, but the language appears to be one never efore encountered in cuneiform. There are no evident links to umerian, Akkadian, Hittite, or any other language known from uneiform inscriptions elsewhere.

s an experiment, I transliterated some of the text into the Roman lphabet, in the hope that it would provide some insight. The first hree lines of panel B, for instance, read as follows:

Fathagan sefak ia ia mana yod sushay evak

Fathagan azar azotot ia ia absimet

Azotot ia ia Vashin vashin ia azotot

Azotot = Azathoth?

That name is better not committed to writing, for reasons which will become clear to you if you accept my invitation to discuss the matter in person.

The name A— that you mentioned, likewise, is better left unspoken and unwritten. I say this not out of superstitious fear, but because dire consequences can result from its reaching the wrong ears or eyes. Despite many attempts down the ages to expunge the name from human knowledge, it is still whispered in some dangerous places by those whose attention it is unwise to attract.

You are correct in what you have surmised about that name; I can add a little to your knowledge, although you will not thank me for doing so. For now, I will say that I find your theory, that the word you transliterated from the cuneiform is a cognate of this name, to be quite plausible.

Only a complete translation of the text will resolve the matter completely. To that end, please visit me in my private apartments at your earliest convenience. You will find me at home most evenings.

Regards,

Henry Armitage.

La'anat – Local Traditions

A wicked city, destroyed by God (Allah) in ancient
. Long before the time of the Prophet, everyone agrees.
Details of the wickedness seem unknown. Some informants
y admit they do not know. Others question my purpose in
ing + state that it is not good to speak of such forbidden things.
The city's name is not remembered, or is remembered as
'anat (Persian, "cursed, forbidden").

All tales agree that the city's people all perished before the
ine wrath that destroyed it. Mortals have been forbidden to
foot there ever since. Some tales of jinn haunting the place—
geys to keep people away.

Extreme horror at the suggestion of setting foot there, even
n pay. The taboo is evidently far stronger than the prospect
f riches, unlike in the royal tombs of Egypt. Extremely
roublesome finding laborers for the excavation. Eventually
arrangements were made to bring them in from distant villages
with no folk memory of the cursed city. While powerful, the
superstition seems localized.